LOCKED OUT OF HEAVEN

(Tomeka's Story—A *Bluesday* Continuation)

Adrienne Thompson

Pink Cashmere Publishing, LLC

Arkansas, USA

Cover art from dreamstime.com

Cover by Adrienne Thompson

Printed in the United States of America

First Printing 2014

Copyright © 2014 Adrienne Thompson

ISBN: 098887136X

ISBN-13: 978-0-9888713-6-6

Thank You, Lord. Just, thank You.

A very special thank you to RedSirens for helping with the English to Spanish translations. Readers, please check out her wonderful jewelry and artwork at: http://www.etsy.com/shop/redsirens

To my readers:

God bless you for your support. I am truly thankful for each and every one of you.

RIP Maya Angelou and Ruby Dee

"It (love) always protects, always trusts, always hopes, always perseveres."

1 Corinthians 13:7

SOUNDTRACK:

"Runaway Baby" Bruno Mars

"Young Girls" Bruno Mars

"If I Knew" Bruno Mars

"Rude Boy" Rihanna

"Man Down" Rihanna

"Crazy In Love" Beyoncé

"Take Care" Drake

"Money Make Her Smile" Bruno Mars

"Swimming Pools" Kendrick Lamar

"Lost In Paradise" Rihanna

"Hunter" Pharrell Williams

"Wake Me Up" Aloe Black

"Searchin' Blues" The Mannish Boys

"Tell Me Mama" Little Walter

"Call On Me" Bobby Blue Bland

"Locked out of Heaven" Bruno Mars

"Grenade" Bruno Mars

"The Other Side" Bruno Mars

"Hold On, We're Going Home" Drake featuring Majid Jordan

"Count On Me" Bruno Mars

SOUNDTRACK CONTINUED:

"Talking to the Moon" Bruno Mars

"It Will Rain" Bruno Mars

"Show Me" Bruno Mars

"Through the window across the room I could see the night sky. I could see a few small stars, and I thought about Arkansas and my old home and my sister and my grandmother. I thought about how badly I used to want to leave there and go away. I was away now. Far away. And I was happy. After sneaking away from my aunt's house, we'd driven all that night and most of the next day until we reached the border."

"Now we were free. No one could tell us what to do. No school or rules for me. I was a woman, an adult, and no one could tell me who to be with. Abraham and I loved each other, and we belonged together. Now nothing and no one could keep us apart."

–Tomeka from Blues In The Key Of B

PROLOGUE

Rio Grande River—Texas/Mexico Border

Present Day...

(Tomeka)

I sat there and tried to catch my breath, but I was too scared to breathe. Too scared to think. I was trembling, but was it from the cold night air that seemed to instantly freeze my wet clothes and skin, or was it from the fear, the terror?

"We gotta keep moving, angel," he said. "Come on, we gotta keep moving. I promise we'll take a break as soon as it's safe."

He reached for my hand and helped me up from the ground. We ran and ran and ran. The sound of the barking dogs made my heart race faster than it already was. *Where did they come from?* I wondered. I hadn't heard them before. And then there were more gun shots. One after the other. I couldn't tell if the shots were coming from Abraham or the other people. I screamed as I covered my ears and continued to run. It was too much. It was all too much. Tears wet my face, almost burning my skin in the freezing cold. I ran until I ran out of both breath and strength. Then I dove into some bushes.

"I'm sorry," I whispered. "I can't run anymore."

No answer. It was then that I realized I was alone. Where was he? Seconds later, I heard a scream. A horrible scream. It was him. They'd caught him.

PART ONE:

MEXICO

(Tomeka)

1

"RUNAWAY BABY"

Mexico City, Mexico

A Few Months Earlier...

I hated it when Abraham left me alone. I hated being closed up in the tiny apartment we shared in Mexico City. I hated how stuffy the air felt, and how small and dark and empty everything seemed when he was gone. I missed his voice and his smile. I missed *him*. I really hated it when he left me behind.

I walked over to the window and watched a group of children playing in the dusty yard outside the apartment building. Mexico City was a huge place full of people and busy streets and skyscrapers—the perfect place to disappear, as Abraham put it. But we were far away from the busy streets and tall, beautiful buildings. We were in the ghetto, if you could call it that. Not quite the slums but not exactly luxury, either—rundown apartments in a rundown neighborhood, living among the poor. Our place wasn't fancy like my Aunt Bobbie's house or even as nice as my granny's little house, but I kept it clean and there weren't many bugs and no rats at all. But the only time this place really felt like home was when Abraham was here. As long as we were together, I wouldn't even mind sleeping in a car. We actually did that a few times as we traveled from Texas to

Mexico City. But I didn't mind. With Abraham's arms around me, I felt safe and sound, like nothing and no one could harm me.

He was out looking for work, afraid we were going to run out of the money he'd saved before he went to jail. That was why we were living in this place, too—to save money. I understood, but I wished we could live somewhere nicer and besides, we hadn't even put a good dent in that money. I knew that to be a fact because I'd counted it for him. We still had $250,000 in American money—more than enough to last us.

I walked into the tiny kitchen, leaned over the sink, and sighed. This was the life I'd chosen. I wanted to be with Abraham and we were together. If it meant I'd have to be a little uncomfortable from time to time, then so be it. There was nothing I wouldn't do to be with him, including living in a rundown apartment. *This* rundown apartment.

I walked over to the couch and sat down. It was times like these, when I was all alone, that I thought of home. Not that I was homesick or anything like that. I didn't miss my granny fussing all the time or my little sister annoying me. No, I wasn't homesick at all. But sometimes I wondered about them, my family. I wondered if Granny was okay, if she was worried about me. But then I remembered how tired of me she always seemed, how she let me miss church and how I was able to keep a phone and write those letters to Abraham without her knowing. As far as I could see, she really didn't care about what I did. No, she couldn't be worried about me.

And my little sister, Sharee? Maybe she missed me like I missed her from time to time. Maybe the whole family missed me. But it'd been five months since I'd left. I was sure they'd all moved on. They probably weren't even looking for me anymore, if they ever had. There was no sense in thinking of home, anyway. Too much had changed. *I* had changed. I didn't sound the same. I didn't talk the same. I didn't even look the same. I was no longer a kid. Well, I was a teenager but I was also a *woman*. I slept with a man every night—*my* man. I was way on the other side of virginity, now, and I had the hips to prove it. No, there was no sense in thinking of home or who might or might not have been looking for me. Mexico was my home. In Mexico, it didn't matter that we were together. In Mexico, we were free. Well, as free as we could be. Abraham wanted me to stay inside. He was afraid of me being noticed or recognized. By who, I had no idea. But I did what he told me to do. I knew he was just concerned because he loved me so much. And I definitely loved him.

I turned on the TV and began to watch my favorite Spanish soap opera. I liked watching those shows because they reminded me of when my granny would watch her stories in the summer time. I never really understood what was going on because I only knew a little Spanish, and that was what Abraham had taught me. But I still liked the soap opera because of the cute guys, beautiful houses, and flashy clothes. And the drama! You don't have to understand every word to know when there's some drama going on. When Abraham was home he would translate for me.

I sighed as I curled my feet under my bottom and continued to watch the TV. I closed my eyes and pictured my Abraham—his brown skin and cold black hair that now hung past his shoulders. I thought about his big brown eyes and his smile that always made my heart jump. And, of course, I thought about his body. Abraham was 5'9" and *fine*. I thought about his voice with its slight accent and the way he said words like bésame and te necesito. Sometimes his voice would make me melt. I would be so glad when he finally made it back home.

***

"Despierta, bella durmiente," Abraham said as he woke me up with a kiss.

I sat up on the sofa and smiled. "What's that mean?"

"Wake up, sleeping beauty."

"Mmm, where've you been so long?" I asked as I reached up and hugged him. He was sweaty. "Ew," I added through a yawn. "You need a shower. What've you been doing?"

He smiled as he pulled his shirt over his head. "Working. At a handbag factory. The hours are long, but they hired me on the spot, so how could I refuse? I missed you, though, cielito." He kissed me again.

"I missed you, too. I'm so glad you're home." I hugged him as tightly as I could. "But you still stink."

He chuckled. "I know. I'm gonna go shower. What's for dinner?"

I only knew how to make three things—fried chicken, fried bacon, and scrambled eggs, and I hadn't even made that for him. Honestly, Abraham usually did most of the cooking for us. "Oh, I fell asleep without cooking. I'm sorry. But I can heat up the corn soup and beans you made yesterday if you want."

He smiled at me. "No hay problema. Come take a shower with me and then we can make dinner together. I'll teach you how to make tamales if we have all of the ingredients. No beans tonight. Remember last night?"

I turned up my nose. "Yeah, I remember! That was so nasty!"

He laughed. "You know you love it when I pass gas."

"I love *you*, but I don't love your gas."

"Ah, come on, cielito. Come help me wash up."

I grinned as he took my hand and pulled me from the couch. I loved it when he gave me cooking lessons, but I loved taking showers with him even more. Then again, I loved doing everything with Abraham.

***

That night as we lay in bed, I looked up at Abraham. His eyes were closed, but I could tell he wasn't asleep. "Abraham?" I whispered.

"Yeah, angel? What's wrong? Not sleepy?"

"No."

"Something on your mind?"

"Yeah... I was wondering if we could go somewhere soon. I haven't really seen the city since we've been here. I wanna ride on the subway and see the tall buildings up close." I knew I was sounding like a little kid, but I couldn't help it. It was hard being closed up in that apartment all of the time.

"Hmm, let me get used to this job, and then I promise to take you out in a couple of weeks. Okay?"

"Could I at least go to the grocery store with you next time?"

He sighed softly. "We'll see. Okay?"

I nodded against his chest. "Okay. Abraham?"

"Yes, angel?"

"I love you."

"I love you, too."

2

"YOUNG GIRLS"

Abraham finally got a day off from work, and that Saturday morning, he got up before me and fixed some scrambled eggs with chorizo. After breakfast, we showered and dressed together, put on baseball caps and dark sunglasses, and left our apartment. I didn't care where he took me. I was just glad he decided to take a chance on letting me leave the apartment.

First, we went to a couple of flea markets where Abraham bought me two really cute dresses and some earrings. Then we went to Walmart to pick up some stuff we needed—deodorant, toilet tissue, toothpaste. We stopped at a street vendor and got some of the best tacos I'd ever tasted in my life! And then Abraham told me he had a surprise for me.

We left the skyscrapers of the city and drove through an older part of town, passing beautiful old buildings of different colors with balconies. Although it was a little cool outside, there were people crowding the sidewalks and cars lining the brick streets. It seemed that many citizens of Ciudad de México were out and about, enjoying the day. Abraham parked his car on the street, opened my door and took my hand, leading me down the sidewalk. We walked hand in hand for a block and then he stopped in front of a building. There were brightly colored drawings on the windows, and the word *tatuaje* was written on the sign that hung over the door.

My eyes widened. "You're gonna get a tattoo?"

He smiled. "Si."

"What are you gonna get?"

He leaned in and kissed me. "You'll see."

We walked inside and while Abraham spoke with the tattoo artist, I walked over to a wall covered with pictures of people and their tattoos since there was no sense in my trying to join their conversation. They were speaking so fast, I couldn't understand a word they said. When it was time for Abraham to get his tattoo, we went into the back of the shop and Abraham laid on his stomach on a table that reminded me of those that were usually found in an examining room in a doctor's office. I sat in a chair close to Abraham's head and held his hand while the tattoo artist went to work on his back. An hour and a half later, my name was etched across the top of his back in huge, fancy letters. It reminded me of Nick Cannon's "Mariah" tattoo.

It was as if my name had been turned into a beautiful work of art. I cried so hard that Abraham thought something was wrong. I told him that I was just happy, that I felt honored that he loved me so much. Abraham sat up on the table and pulled me to him, kissing me all over my face and whispering in Spanish and English that he loved me.

"I want one, too," I said.

Abraham rubbed his thumbs over my cheeks, wiping away my tears. "You want some ink, angel? You sure?"

I nodded. "I'm sure."

I was too scared to get a big tattoo, so I decided to get the letter "A" tattooed on the inside of my right wrist. I chose that spot because that was where my skin was lightest. I was afraid it might not show up anywhere else. I used to get teased sometimes for being so dark skinned when I was little. The kids in elementary school would call me all sorts of crazy names. But Abraham said that my skin was his favorite part of me. He liked how it looked next to his. I can't lie, though. Getting a tattoo in that spot really hurt, but I was glad I did it. Now, I would always have a piece of Abraham with me.

"Now we'll always be together, no matter what," Abraham said once we climbed back into the car.

"Yeah, we will," I replied.

We grabbed a couple more tacos on our way home and then we spent the rest of the day in bed. It was one of the best days of my entire life.

***

What I missed most about my old life was having someone to talk to sometimes. I mean, sure, I had Abraham to talk to when he was home and not too tired to listen. But sometimes, I wished I had a friend or two to talk to—someone to share my feelings with. I got so lonely staying in that apartment day after day all by myself. I even kind of missed school, or at least I missed seeing my friends. Like Myasha, who was always cutting up in class. Or T'nay, who fell in love with a different boy every week—or at least that's how it seemed. It was kind of crazy that I was thinking about them, though.

I hadn't seen them since me and Granny and Sharee left Arkansas.

I also missed basketball games and pep rallies. I even missed church. Abraham and I hadn't been to church since we left Texas, but he made sure we read a scripture from the Bible and prayed together every Sunday morning. Not that I wasn't happy with him. Like I said, I was *very* happy with him. It's just that my life was so... different. And there were just some things I really missed.

I sat there on the sofa and stared at the TV like I did every single day. I sighed and tried to tell myself that Abraham would be home soon, but I knew that was a lie. In the two weeks since he'd started working at that factory, he'd been coming home later and later. Sometimes he worked sixteen hours in one day and when he made it home, he barely ate or said a word to me. He just climbed into bed and fell asleep. Those nights, he didn't touch me at all. And I hated that more than anything.

A knock at the door almost made me jump out of my skin. I didn't know any of the other people who lived in the building or in all of Mexico City for that matter. I hardly ever walked outside and when I did, I made sure not to talk to anyone. So who was at the door? I sat there and listened to whoever it was knock two more times. I held my breath, half-expecting a cop to kick the door in. My heart raced as I stood from the couch and slowly walked to the door. Then I heard a soft, timid voice. "¿Hay alguien en casa?"

I had no idea what the woman on the other side of my door said other than the word casa which I knew meant house or home, but she definitely didn't sound like a cop. I unlocked and slowly opened the door. Standing there was a girl, probably my age, wearing jeans and a t-shirt, holding an empty cup in her hand. Standing next to her was a little boy. He was tiny with big brown eyes. I smiled.

"¿Tiene agua? No tenemos agua," she said.

I shook my head. "No hablo Español," I repeated one of the few phrases I'd learned from Abraham. "Yo hablo Inglés."

Her face lit up. "Are you American?"

I nodded. "Yes. You speak English?"

Her head bobbed up and down so fast, I was afraid she'd hurt herself. "¡Si! Yes! I am Maribel. This is my little brother, Marco. Our water is not working. Do you have some water? Enough to fill this cup for my brother?"

I hesitated, peered behind her to be sure this wasn't a trick or a trap or something, and then opened the door wider. "Sure. Come on in."

She smiled and gently pushed her little brother forward. His eyes were wide as he slowly walked into my apartment. I smiled at him then squatted next to him. "It's okay," I said.

He smiled and looked up at his sister who nodded at him. Once they were both inside, I closed and locked the door. I stood there for a second, still unsure if what I was doing was right and scared that Abraham would come home and be angry with me for taking a chance like this. But more than that, I was scared of being found and taken away from him. Because, though life with him was hard, I didn't even want to think about living life without him.

I looked at her and then at the empty cup in her hand. "Oh, the water," I remembered. I led her into the kitchen and turned the faucet on. She placed the cup under the stream of water and then handed it to her brother who gulped it down so fast, I thought he'd choke. He looked up at her and said something in Spanish that I couldn't understand. She shook her head and answered him in Spanish. Then she turned to me.

"Thank you," she said with a smile.

As she turned to leave, I said, "Wait! Um, does he want some more?"

She shook her head. "No, it's okay. He's had enough."

"What about you? Do you want some water, too?"

She held onto the cup and dropped her eyes. "No."

I knew she was lying. "Wait a second," I said.

She nodded and took her brother's hand. I grabbed a big pot and filled it with water then I handed it to her. "Here, take this with you. You can come back for some more tomorrow."

She smiled brightly. "Are you sure? Will your husband mind?"

I frowned. "Husband? Oh, Abraham? Um, just come around one tomorrow afternoon. He'll be at work."

She smiled again. "Okay. Gracias—I mean, thank you. Um, what is your name?"

"Oh, um… uh-um, Meka." I just couldn't think of a fake name to give her. In all the months we'd been in Mexico, Abraham and I had never even talked about a fake name for me because I wasn't supposed to go anywhere without him or talk to anyone or let anyone in our apartment. I wasn't even supposed to answer the door.

"Okay, Meka. We will see you tomorrow."

They walked out of my apartment to the apartment right next door. She waved as she opened her door. I waved back and then ducked back inside. I closed and locked the door and smiled a little smile. *I think that maybe I just made a friend.*

***

"Te amo tanto," Abraham said as he reached across the bed, pulled me close to him, and kissed me.

I smiled and snuggled closely to him. "I love you more."

He grinned as he tapped the tip of my nose with his finger. "You are learning so fast, angel! Soon, you'll be speaking Spanish better than me."

"Not hardly. I just know a little bit." What I didn't say was that Maribel had been teaching me Spanish every day while he was gone to work. In three weeks, my Spanish vocabulary had really grown.

"Well, one day we'll be able to go back to the US, so you won't have to worry about it."

I leaned up on my elbow and looked at him. "For real?"

He reached up and rubbed his finger across my lips. "Yes. I know you're not happy here. I'm not either. I know you miss your family."

I dropped my eyes. "As long as we're together, I'm okay. I don't have to see them."

"Meka, you don't have to lie to me. I know you miss them. I miss mine, too. I'm gonna make a way for us to go home. I promise you that. But it'll take time. I violated my parole. Things are too hot back in Texas for me right now and we'll need to wait until you're eighteen. That way no one can make you stay. You can leave when you want and we can stay together." He leaned up and kissed me.

I smiled. "I love you, Abraham."

"I love you, too, cielito. More than you will ever know. If anyone ever tries to hurt you, I'll hurt them. There's nothing I won't do for you. I'd die for you."

"I'd die for you, too."

"Do you ever think of home or your family?"

I nodded as I reached over and hugged him again. "I do. I think about my Granny and the rest of my family. Sometimes I wonder what they're doing and if they miss me. I even think about my father from time to time. And then there are other things I think about that really bother me so I try not to think about them."

He hugged me tightly. "Like what, angel?"

I sighed, hesitated a little, and then said, "Like why my parents didn't care enough to raise me and my sister and why my dad killed my mother. I mean, she wasn't perfect, but I don't think she deserved to die. I can still see her face from time to time. She was pretty. Sharee looks so much like her.

"Sometimes I wonder why my mother's family never tried to have anything to do with me and my sister. They never came to see us or anything. The first and only time I ever even saw them was at the memorial service my aunt had for my mother. And all they said was, 'Y'all done got so big.' That was it. And they never tried to see us again."

"I'm sorry, angel."

"It's okay. I just wonder why God let so much bad stuff happen to me. I just don't understand what I did to deserve it."

He softly kissed my cheek. "You didn't do anything. I used to always hear my grandmother say that God gives us what He knows we can handle. He knew you could handle it. And besides, there's been some good in your life, too, right? Your granny and your aunt and uncle?"

I smiled. "And you. You are the best part of my life."

He smiled at me and then he kissed me for a long time. I kissed him back and we held each other tightly. Then we loved each other for the rest of the night.

3

"IF I KNEW"

It was a little after four in the afternoon and I was beginning to worry about Maribel. Since we'd first met, she hadn't missed a day of coming over for water and a Spanish lesson. She was nice and friendly and I really liked her. But I also worried about her. She wore the same clothes every day and the same shoes—no coat, and it was getting chilly outside. And she and Marco seemed to get skinnier and skinnier by the day. Sometimes, they would eat lunch with me. Other times, she'd be in a hurry to get back home, like she was afraid of being caught outside her apartment. I never saw or met her parents, and she never mentioned them. I didn't ask her about them because I didn't want her to ask me about my life. So I was left to wonder and worry, because there was something obviously wrong. Why didn't they have water? Did they have food? I thought about those things a lot, probably more than I should have.

I wanted to ask Abraham if we could buy Maribel's family some food or help them with their water. We still had all of that money saved up in a suitcase under the bed—Abraham's money from before he went to prison. But he still wouldn't spend it. He said it was our back-up money and we were just going to live off of the money he made at the factory. But Maribel was my friend and as scared as I was of upsetting Abraham, I was very concerned about her.

I opened the door a little and peeked out. I could hear bolero music blasting from a car's stereo. The sun was warm despite the chilliness in the air, and the brightness nearly blinded me. I didn't get out in the sun enough. I really didn't, but I was trying to do what Abraham told me to. I was trying to stay out of sight—from the police and the drug dealers, both of which—according to him—were equally dangerous.

He was sure that the authorities were still looking for me and that, by now, they had probably figured out that we were in Mexico. Our faces were probably plastered on every missing person's website on the internet, according to him. Maybe he was right. I might've been on the back of a milk carton by now. It was going on seven months since I left my family back in Texas. It probably wasn't safe for me to show my face.

And then there were the drug dealers, who basically ran the streets of Mexico City. They did what they wanted when they wanted to do it—including shooting anyone that got in their way. There was no way Abraham could have put his money in a bank, but keeping it in the apartment was very dangerous. If anyone, anyone at all, in this rundown apartment complex knew how much money we had stashed away, they'd kick the door in and take it. And if I happened to get in the way, they'd run right over me.

Abraham had drilled these things into my head and he'd scared me to death. I was scared when I opened the door and peeked outside, scared when the hot sun hit my face. Scared when the little kids that were playing outside turned and looked at me like I was a ghost or something. But as scared as I was, I was even more worried about my friend—my *only* friend.

I closed the door and leaned against it. I shut my eyes and took a deep breath. I walked across the room, slipped on a pair of flip-flop sandals, and then walked back over to the door and opened it. I walked outside and nearly ran the five footsteps that separated her apartment from mine. I glanced around and knocked on the door. My hand was shaking so hard that I knocked three times instead of the two I'd intended. I stood and waited, my eyes darting right then left. I tapped my foot and closed my eyes. *Please hurry up and answer the door, Maribel. Please.*

I knocked again, glanced around some more, held my breath, and then, *finally*, the door slowly opened a crack and Maribel squinted at me. "Meka?" she said weakly.

"Yeah. What happened? I was waiting for you to come over. You don't need any water?"

She slowly shook her head. "No."

I frowned. She looked tired and weak, and I didn't hear or see her brother. But then again, I couldn't see much at all since the door was barely open. "Where's Marco? Does he want some water?"

She closed her eyes and the next thing I knew, she was falling. I caught her and, at the same time, the door flew open. And what I saw almost made me cry. The apartment was empty—no furniture, no pictures on the walls, no TV, no nothing except for some newspapers piled up in the middle of the floor. Marco was lying on top of them, asleep.

I was still holding on to Maribel as I walked into their apartment and shut the door. It felt colder in that apartment than it did outside. At that moment, I understood what people meant when they said they were chilled to the bone. It was freezing in there!

I dragged her over to where Marco was and laid her down beside him. Then I stood there and tried to figure out what to do or who to call. I couldn't think. I just stood there and stared at Maribel and Marco and then I started crying. *Think, think.*

I had a cell phone—a burner for emergencies, for if I needed to call Abraham when he was away from home. Wasn't this an emergency? I hurried out the door and back to my own apartment and grabbed my phone. I dialed Abraham's number and nervously waited for him to answer while peeking out the front door.

He didn't answer, so I left a message. "Abraham? It's me, it's Meka. Call me back, please. I need your help. *Hurry*."

I took the phone with me next door and checked on my friend and her brother again. They were both breathing, but they were still asleep. I walked through the apartment, looking for—I don't know what I was looking for. An answer? An explanation of what was going on? The apartment was exactly the same as mine and Abraham's except there was no furniture and the lights didn't work. I checked every switch in every room—nothing. The kitchen was empty except for a few empty potato chip sacks and candy wrappers that were piled on the floor in a corner. The refrigerator was empty and it smelled musty. But if it had been full of food, the food would've spoiled because it wasn't on either. When I turned the handle on the faucet, there was no water.

There was no sign that anyone else lived there. Didn't she have parents? Now I wished I'd asked her more about her life instead of being so worried about hiding mine. When my phone rang, I nearly dropped it. My hand was shaking again when I pressed the button to accept the call.

"Hello? Abraham?"

"Meka! Meka, what's wrong—what's going on?! I left work. I'm on my way home right now. Did something happen to you?"

"No, not me. It's… it's my friend."

There was silence, and then he said, "What friend? Meka, where are you?"

I tried not to cry, but I couldn't help it. I sniffled and wiped tears from my face. "I'm… I'm next door. Something is wrong with my friend and her brother."

"Next door? Friend? What are you doing next door? What is going on? Did someone come into our apartment?"

"N… no. Maribel, she's my friend. She, she teaches me Spanish when you go to work. Something is wrong with her. She's sick, Abraham. You have to help her."

Click.

I thought he'd hung up on me until I heard footsteps on the landing outside of the apartment and then I heard Abraham's voice. "Meka! Meka!" he whispered loudly.

I snatched the door to Maribel's apartment open. "In here!"

The first thing he did when he walked into the apartment was to grab me and hug me tightly. "You scared me, cielito! I thought something had happened to you. Don't scare me like that! I thought one of the drug dealers around here had gotten to you."

I shook my head and backed away from him. "No." I looked over at my friend and her brother then back at Abraham. "They need our help."

He kneeled beside them and laid a hand on each of them. He looked up at me. "The little boy is gone."

I frowned and fell to the floor beside them. "No… no. He was breathing. I just checked. *No.*" I placed a hand on his chest then over his mouth. Nothing. I clamped my hand over my mouth and moaned as tears filled my eyes. "*No.* Why? I don't understand… why?"

Abraham grabbed me and held onto me. "How well did you know him?"

"I've known them for a few weeks, I think. They would come over for water every day. Sometimes I'd give them food. I don't think they had any. He was a good boy. I just don't understand what's going on. Where are their parents? Is… is she…"

He rubbed my hair. "No, she's alive. If they didn't have food or water, he probably starved to death."

"Oh, God. I should've given them more. I should've helped more."

"Shh," he said as he continued to hold me. "Let me call for some help."

I nodded as he let go of me and pulled out his phone.

"And then, Meka, we've got to leave here. And we've got to leave *tonight*."

"But if we leave, I'll never know what happened to her. Can't we just—"

He shook his head. "These kids are squatters. This is not their home. That's why there's no food, no electricity, no furniture. They probably broke in here. Or worse, this is their home and their parents left them here to fend for themselves. Either way, the cops are going to be crawling all over this place, asking questions, trying to find out what happened. We've got to leave, Meka. As soon as I make this call, we've got to pack up and go. Do you understand?"

I stared down at Maribel and slowly nodded. "Yes."

He pulled out his phone and made the call, speaking entirely in Spanish. I only recognized a few words, including: enfermo—sick, and el hospital—hospital, of course. Oh, and rápido—*fast*.

He hung up his phone and reached for my hand as I stood there and stared at Maribel. "Come on, Meka."

I didn't move and I didn't take his hand. "But—"

"Meka! We've got to go. We've got to go, *now*!"

"Wait," I said. I ran to our apartment, grabbed a blanket, and ran back next door. I covered both Maribel and Marco up and whispered, "Bye." Then I took Abraham's hand.

We left, closing the door behind us. Inside our apartment, Abraham grabbed two suitcases—the one that was full of money and another one that we always kept packed in case we needed to leave in a hurry. It had some of our clothes and deodorant and stuff like that in it. My job was to gather up some food to take with us. I knew that because we'd been over and over what we would do in a case like this. So, while Abraham raced to the car with our bags, I shoved as much food as I could into a duffel bag. When he came back to the apartment, he took the bag from me and with his other hand, grabbed mine and pulled me out of the apartment, past the closed door of my friend's apartment, and down the rusty metal stairs to his car. Once I climbed inside, I began to cry. As we left, an ambulance and a police car roared past us.

4

"RUDE BOY"

It was dark and several hours had passed before Abraham pulled into a motel parking lot. I was tired but my mind was too jumbled up to sleep. I was worried about Maribel and I was sad about her brother. I was also sad for me and Abraham. We had made a life in Mexico City. It wasn't perfect, but at least we had our own place. I hated to think of the money he'd wasted buying the furniture we'd just left behind like it was trash. And now he'd have to do it all over again.

"Where are we?" I asked as he turned the engine off.

"Guadalajara. Stay here. I'll be right back."

I nodded and watched as he left the car and walked into the motel office. I sat up in my seat and looked around. It was an okay motel, I guessed. There were a lot of cars in the parking lot. I sighed. What did it matter where we stayed? I was with Abraham. That was all that mattered. I closed my eyes and laid my head against the seat. I would just be glad to get out of the car and into the shower and then into bed with my man.

Tap, tap, tap.

My eyes popped open and I turned my head to see a man standing next to the car, staring at me. He said something to me in Spanish that I didn't understand. Then he made a motion for me to let my window down. I turned and looked at the office, silently wishing that Abraham would hurry up. I looked back at the man and shook my head, no.

He spoke again, louder this time. He was yelling something that I still couldn't understand. My eyes darted back to the office. Still no sign of Abraham. My heart was racing as I turned and shook my head again. This time, the man took his fist and banged on the window. I let out a shriek. And finally, Abraham appeared. He walked around to my side of the car and faced the man and they began arguing in Spanish.

I slapped my hand against the window and shouted, "Abraham!"

He glanced at me for a moment and then turned back to the man in time to dodge a punch. Abraham swung at the man and landed his punch square against the man's jaw.

"Abraham!" I shouted again.

The man fell and Abraham kicked him... over and over again. I rolled my window down a couple of inches. "Abraham!"

He turned and looked at me but he never stopped kicking the man. Tears began to fill my eyes and my voice trembled as I repeated his name one more time, "*Abraham*."

And he stopped. He backed away from the man who didn't move a muscle. He just... he just laid there like he was... like he was dead. Abraham spat on the man before leaving him there on the pavement and climbing back into the car with me.

My cheeks were wet when he reached over and kissed me. "I'm sorry. I don't like to lose control like that. But he had it coming."

I looked over at the man again. "Is he... is he dead?"

Abraham shrugged as he started the car. "I don't know. I don't think so."

"Why… what did he say to make you so mad?"

Abraham sighed as he drove toward our room. "He wanted to know how much it would cost to sleep with you."

I gasped. "What?!"

"I told him to get lost or I was gonna kick his ass. I guess he didn't believe me."

I didn't ask him any more questions. After I took my shower, I climbed into bed with him without eating any dinner. I couldn't get that man out of my mind or the way Abraham had beaten him. The look on Abraham's face was so scary. It was like he was another person. I closed my eyes and tried to forget what had happened. But the man's face was only replaced by Maribel's and Marco's faces. I don't think I slept at all that night.

***

The next morning I sat on the side of the bed in our motel room and stared down at the paper plate in my lap. Huevos rancheros had become my favorite breakfast food during my time in Mexico, but right at that moment, I might as well have been holding a plate full of slop.

"What's wrong? You not hungry? Shoot, I can't believe that. You're *always* hungry. Where you putting all that food? In those hips? 'Cause ain't nothing else changed. You're still my tall, skinny, brown angel." Abraham grinned as he chewed his food.

I didn't smile back at him.

"Come on, baby. It tastes pretty good to me. Got it from a restaurant down the street. And I spent a lot of money on it—forty-five pesos." He gave me a wink.

I shook my head. "No, I'm not hungry." I looked up at him. "And I know that's only about three dollars."

He sat his plate on the bed. "You still upset about the guy I beat up last night? He deserved it. Actually, he deserved worse. I shoulda stomped his brains in, make sure he can't say no stupid crap like that again. "

I pushed the food around on my plate with a plastic fork. "It's not just that. I'm worried about my friend."

Abraham sighed. "Look, Meka. We did what we could do for her. You saw the ambulance. I'm sure they helped her."

"I just wish I could see her again. She was my friend. My only friend in Mexico."

"Yeah, well, she shouldn't have been your friend. You should've kept to yourself like I told you to. Now look where we are—a musty motel room instead of our own place. Got to start over *again*."

"I was-I was lonely."

"Do you want to be with me, Meka? I mean, do you *really* want to be with me?" he asked in a stern voice.

I looked up at him and frowned. "Yes. Why are you asking me that? You *know* I want to be with you!"

"Because I just don't know anymore. If you really want to be with me, you're going to have to stop worrying about having friends or someone to talk to. You're not a little girl anymore. You're a woman—*my* woman. And I need for my woman to listen to me and to trust me and to do what I tell her to do." He stood from his side of the bed and walked around to mine. "Do you trust me, Meka? Do you trust me to take care of you and watch out for you? Cuz that's all I'm tryna do."

I looked up at him as he reached down and rubbed my cheek with his rough hand. I took his hand and kissed it. "Yes."

He kneeled in front of me and looked me in the eye. "Then you've got to do what I tell you to do *all the time*. No exceptions. Okay?"

I looked into the eyes of the first and only man I'd ever loved in my short life and nodded. "Okay. I'm sorry. But—"

He placed a finger against my lips and said, "Shh. No buts." He kissed me for a long moment. "Now, what do I have to do to make you smile?"

I shrugged.

"You don't know? How about this." He kissed my neck.

I smiled a little.

"Or this." He stood up and pulled me to my feet then hugged me tightly.

I leaned against him and smiled.

"I love you, Meka."

"I love you, too."

We stood there for a while and I wished he'd never let me go. "I really am sorry for causing us so much trouble. I bet you wish you were still with your old girlfriend now."

He looked down at me and shook his head. "No, I don't. I haven't even thought about her since we've been together."

"Didn't you love her?"

"I cared about her, but I've never loved anyone like I love you. You saved me when I was locked up, angel. If it hadn't been for you, I wouldn't have made it."

I smiled as I closed my eyes and squeezed my arms around him. "You saved me, too."

"Hey," he whispered. "You wanna get married?"

I backed away from him and with wide eyes said, "Can we do that? I'm still not eighteen."

He shrugged. "We don't have to do it legally. We could just go to a church and ask a preacher to do it. It'll be official in the eyes of God. That's all that matters."

I was smiling so hard that my cheeks began to hurt. "Yes! I wanna get married."

He kissed me again. "Then get dressed so we can go get some rings. It should be easy to find a church around here."

I was grinning from ear to ear as I said, "Okay!"

5

"MAN DOWN"

Abraham and I were married in a tiny church in Guadalajara, Mexico, surrounded by rickety wooden pews and ancient statues of Jesus and The Virgin Mary. The preacher was a tiny man with leathery, wrinkled skin and weak, gray eyes. He wore dingy overalls and held what had to be the oldest Bible in the world in his hands. He had to lean on a cane at the altar and performed the entire ceremony in Spanish. Abraham had to tell me when to say "I do." The only witness was an older lady who happened to be inside the church when we got there.

When the preacher pronounced us man and wife—or at least I guess that's what he said—Abraham smiled down at me and kissed me for what felt like hours. Then he pulled me into the tightest hug and whispered in my ear, "My angel. I love you, Señora Rios."

"I love you, too, Señor Rios," I replied.

On the way back to our room, Abraham stopped at a store and bought us some tres leches cake and two bottles of Sol beer to celebrate. It would be my first time drinking beer and I was so excited!

When we made it back to our motel room, the first thing Abraham did was dump his box of condoms in the trash. "You're my wife now. We don't need these anymore," he said.

I smiled as he took me into his arms and kissed me long and hard.

We undressed each other and for the first time, made love as husband and wife. That night was absolutely magical.

**

Bang! Bang! Bang!

I sat up straight in the bed at the sound of someone knocking, no, *kicking* against the door to our room. I looked over at Abraham who held a finger to his lips as he pulled on his underwear. "Angel, go in the bathroom, lock the door behind you, and don't come out until I tell you to," he whispered, his breath still smelling like beer and cake.

I nodded and, on shaky legs, quietly darted into the bathroom, locking the door behind me. I grabbed a towel from the rack and wrapped it around my naked body. I sat on the toilet, closed my eyes, and silently prayed that it wasn't the police who were at the door. I didn't want to be taken away from Abraham. I loved him so much, and we were married now. We were one. We were *supposed* to be together.

The banging continued, and though I was further away from it, it seemed louder. I heard Abraham shout something in Spanish. I was tempted to open the door, but I knew he couldn't have been talking to me. If he was talking to me, he would make sure I understood him.

More banging, then a loud crash and a thud. Then lots of yelling in Spanish—not just Abraham, but other voices. Men's voices. I stood and leaned against the door.

Abraham.

Please God, let him be okay. Please.

Yelling, crashing, thumping. Several minutes passed. My stomach churned. My heart was beating so fast, I just knew it was going to stop. And then I heard something that almost made me pee on myself. *A gunshot.* And then it was quiet. No more crashes or thuds or voices. *Nothing.* I started crying before I even realized it.

Abraham.

Was he... was he dead?

I leaned against the door and cried. I was too scared to open it. What was I going to do if he was dead? What was I going to do? How was I going to go on living without him? I couldn't. I couldn't live without him. There was no way I could. I looked down at the wedding band Abraham had slid on my finger just a few hours earlier and wailed softly.

"Angel..."

I stopped crying. Had I really just heard that? Or was I imagining it?

"Angel, you can come out now." His voice was soft and he sounded like it hurt him to talk.

I unlocked the door and slowly opened it. What I saw on the other side of that door looked like something out of a nightmare or a movie. The two chairs and table that sat in the corner of the room were broken and the splintered pieces were scattered everywhere. The covers had been snatched off of the bed. The door was lying flat on the floor like a long, wooden welcome mat. The heat was on but the open door let all of the cold air in. I rubbed my hands over my arms as my eyes darted around the room trying to take it all in.

Trying to figure out what happened.

There were people peering into the room saying things I didn't understand. Some looked concerned; others were taking pictures or, maybe, videos, with cell phones. I adjusted the towel that was wrapped around me and then stepped over to the doorway and lifted the door, which wasn't as heavy as it looked, and placed it in the doorway. I kind of leaned it into the door facing since the hinges were broken. At least now, it would be a little harder for people to see inside the room.

"Meka..."

Abraham.

I carefully walked through the rubble and found Abraham lying on the floor on the other side of the bed. There was blood everywhere—like someone had exploded.

"Abraham!" I shrieked. "Are you hurt?! Is this all your blood?!"

I looked down at where he gripped his right leg with both hands. "Grab the sheet over there," he said, not really answering my question.

I quickly searched the room with my eyes and found the sheet. I handed it to him.

"Help me. Hold my leg."

I nodded and, with shaky hands, held his leg while he ripped the sheet and tied part of it around the spot where I could see blood oozing out of a hole. Tears fell from my eyes, and with a sniffle, I said, "Do you... do you need to go to the hospital?"

He shook his head. "No, it went through my leg, through the muscle. I don't think it hit the bone. But we gotta get outta here before the police arrive. Put on some clothes and grab our bags. I think I can drive."

Abraham stumbled to his feet and sat on the side of the bed. I ran into the bathroom, washed my bloody hands, and got dressed then rushed back into the room, grabbed our bags, and followed Abraham out to the car after he knocked the door back down to the floor. He was breathing heavily and sweating like he'd just run a marathon. Once he'd started the car and screeched out of the parking lot, I said, "What happened back there? Who... who shot you?"

"The guy I beat up on the parking lot the other night. He came looking for payback. And he brought a couple of friends with him. I shoulda killed him when I had the chance. That's what I get for trying to show him some mercy. I just hated to kill him in front of you, you know?"

I sat in the passenger seat with tears rolling down my face as Abraham raced through Guadalajara to the highway on the way to— I had no idea where we were headed and I didn't ask. I was too scared to ask. Too scared to do anything but cry.

"I need a damn gun," he whispered.

I just sat there and cried until I cried myself to sleep.

***

When I woke up in the car, I wasn't sure where we were. There was nothing but darkness around us—no street lights, no headlights, nothing. As a matter of fact, the only light at all was the moonlight. I wiped my eyes and yawned as I looked around. We were parked on the side of the road and all I could make out was desert, more desert, and a long stretch of highway. And it was so cold. I looked over at Abraham who was sitting behind the wheel, fast asleep. I reached over and gently touched his cheek. His face was so wet. It was too cold for him to be sweating like that. Was he sick? I turned and looked out the back window. Not a car in sight. We were totally alone, and I think that scared me as much as if we were being chased.

I shook Abraham gently. He moaned softly but didn't wake up. I leaned close to him. "Abraham."

No answer.

I put my hand on his thigh and kissed his cheek. "Abraham, where are we?"

His eyelids slowly opened and he looked over at me and smiled. "Angel. I was just dreaming about you."

I smiled. "Where are we?"

"Hmm, the middle of nowhere."

"Why are we here? On the side of the road."

He turned and placed his blood-stained hand on my cheek. "My leg. I needed to rest. I'm okay now." He kissed me.

I placed my hand on top of his and kissed him back. "How's your leg?"

"It's okay. It hurts but not too bad. Just need to wake up good, then we can hit the road again."

"Okay. Are you sure you don't need a doctor? You're... you're sweating. And you lost a lot of blood."

"No, I can't take that chance. Just pray for me, angel. I know your prayers go straight to God's ears."

I nodded and leaned back in my seat. "I always pray for you."

Abraham reached over and rested his hand on my thigh. "Are you okay?"

I shook my head. "I'm scared."

He squeezed my thigh. "Don't be scared. I'm not gonna let anything happen to you. I'ma always take care of you. I'd die for you. Remember?"

"That's what I'm scared of. I don't think I could keep living if something happened to you, Abraham. I love you too much."

"Don't say that, angel. If something happens to me, you *gotta* keep living. You hear me?" He leaned over and kissed me so deeply, I almost couldn't breathe. "You hear me, Meka?"

"You can't die, then."

"I'm not planning on it."

"Good."

He reached for my hand and squeezed it in his and we sat there for a minute in complete silence. I closed my eyes and was almost asleep when Abraham said, "You know what we haven't ever done?"

I frowned a little and shook my head. "No. What?"

He grinned. "We haven't done it in a car."

"Done what?"

"*It.*"

"Ohhh, can you... can you do it, with your leg like that?"

"I can if you do the work. Come sit in my lap."

"Is there enough room with the steering wheel?"

He let his seat back. "Now there is."

"What if a car passes by? What if they see us?"

"Good. Let them see us. Let them see me making love to my wife. I don't care."

I giggled as I pulled off my jeans and climbed into his lap.

6

"CRAZY IN LOVE"

Some hours later, we made it to Durango, Mexico. Abraham had bled through his pants and I had to help him change them in the car before he could go and get us a room. When we finally unlocked the door to our motel room and walked inside, Abraham sat on the bed and I helped him clean his leg and we wrapped one of his t-shirts around it. The bleeding had slowed down a lot, thank goodness. After we had finished, Abraham lay back in the bed and closed his eyes.

As much as I hated to bother him, I had to tell him. "I'm hungry, Abraham." We'd been in such a hurry, we'd left all of our food back in Guadalajara.

He opened one eye and looked at me. "I saw a Subway up the street. Get me something, too." He dug in his pocket and handed me some money. "Don't talk to anyone, Meka. Get the food and come right back. You're probably all over YouTube in that towel by now."

I gasped. "You think so?!"

"Probably. Put on my shades, too."

I nodded. I turned to leave and he said, "Come here." I walked over to him and he pulled me close, kissed my cheek. "Be careful, angel. And hurry back."

"I will."

I took the room key and tucked it in the pocket of my jeans as I left the room. I adjusted Abraham's shades on my face as I began the walk to Subway. I could see the sign from our room. It was less than a block away, but I was so nervous and scared, I wasn't sure if I would make it. It was a clear morning and the walk could have been a nice one but there were so many thoughts in my mind. So much had happened in such a short amount of time. I was tired and scared and worried—worried about Abraham's leg. Worried about my face being plastered all over YouTube. What if the incident made the news? What if someone recognized us? What if the authorities were in Guadalajara right now, checking for fingerprints? What if someone saw what direction we went in when we left? What if they were on the way to Durango right now? What if someone in Subway recognized me?

That did it. Before I made it to Subway, I turned around and went back to the motel, to our room. Abraham was fast asleep when I climbed into bed with him. I snuggled closely to him and buried my face in his chest. I felt him move.

He looked down at me and said, "Where's the food?"

"I changed my mind. I'm not that hungry. I can eat later."

He wrapped his arm around me. "My leg hurts kinda bad right now."

I sat up. "It does? What do you need? Some medicine?"

"I need something to take my mind off of it. Something like what we did in the car."

I rolled my eyes and lay back down. "I don't see how that's gonna help."

"It will. *Please*." He kissed me softly. "Lo necesito, baby."

I laid there for a second and tried not to smile. "Okay."

***

We'd made it to Durango in the middle of that morning. I didn't wake up until the middle of that night to a grumbling stomach and a dry mouth. It had been hours since I'd eaten and I regretted turning back from Subway. I eased Abraham's arm from my waist and slid out of bed. I remembered seeing some vending machines near the motel office. At least I could get some chips and a soda. Maybe that would quiet my growling stomach.

I pulled on my clothes, grabbed the key, and quietly left the room, leaving Abraham asleep in bed. There wasn't a soul in sight as I made my way to the machines. I bought two bags of chips, two sodas, and two candy bars just in case Abraham was hungry, too. When I turned around to head back to our room, there was a man standing behind me. I jumped, dropping my food in the process. The man stared at me. My heart thumped in my chest. Then he smiled and bent down to pick my stuff up. When he handed it to me, I said, "Gracias."

He nodded. "De nada."

I hurried back to the room and slammed the door shut, waking Abraham. He sat straight up in the bad. "Where've you been?!" he shrieked.

"To the vending machine. I got hungry. I brought you something, too."

I walked over to him. His skin was pale and his eyes looked so weak. I placed my hand on his forehead like my granny would do when me or Sharee would get sick. "You got a fever. You're sick, Abraham."

He took my hand and kissed it. "Lovesick."

I smiled as I crawled into the bed next to him. "You hungry?"

He scooted up in the bed, breathing hard as he leaned against the headboard. "I could eat."

We sat together, munching on chips and guzzling soda. I was eating my candy bar when Abraham reached for my hand and squeezed it. His hand felt so warm. "I love you, angel."

"I love you, too."

"If I can walk on this leg in the morning, I'm gonna go get us some real food."

"I can... I can do it."

"No, I shouldn't have let you go to Subway. Your face is probably on one of those cell phones. It's too risky for you to be out in public."

I nodded. "Abraham, I think you need to let a doctor look at your leg. I'm worried about you."

"I'm tough, baby. Can't no bullet stop me. Stop worrying." He pulled me to him and I closed my eyes. In no time, I'd fallen asleep again.

7

"TAKE CARE"

I woke up around ten the next morning in a hot, empty room. At first I thought that maybe Abraham was in the bathroom, but he wasn't. I looked outside the window and saw that his car was gone. I sat on the side of the bed and sighed. I guessed he was out getting us some breakfast. By noon, he still hadn't made it back and on top of starving, I was beginning to worry about him. What if something had happened to him? If he'd been arrested, he'd never tell the police where I was. How long was I supposed to wait? What was I supposed to do?

I lay across the bed and buried my face in the covers and cried. When the maid knocked on the door, I sent her away and kept crying. By two o'clock, I was sure I'd never see my Abraham, my husband, my *love*, again. Exhausted from worry and hungrier than I'd ever been in my life, I finally drifted off to sleep again.

I woke up around 1:00 AM. Still no Abraham, but there was a Subway sack on the little table by the window. It had been sitting there in the heat of the room so long, the cheese had melted on the cold cut sandwich and the cold cuts were lukewarm. I was too hungry to care. I assumed that Abraham had been in and out of the room while I was asleep. I ate the sandwich in record time then drank the warm can of soda that also sat on the table. Then I sat there and tried not to cry. At least I knew he was okay, at least I knew he hadn't been arrested. But where was he and what was he doing?

I sat there a few minutes longer and then decided to take a shower because I definitely needed one. I hadn't had one since long before we left Guadalajara. The water felt so good, I didn't want to get out of that shower. I wished I could've stood there all night and day and let that water wash over me. I closed my eyes and let the water cover my face and hair. I hadn't had my hair pressed since before I left home, and now it was a bushy, hard-to-manage mess, but Abraham said he loved it.

When I took my head from under the water, I thought I heard a noise. I froze. Was someone else in the room?

"Abraham?!" I called.

Nothing.

I turned the water off. "Abraham?!"

Silence.

I stood there and listened for a full minute.

Then someone snatched the shower curtain back and grabbed me from behind. As I tried to scream, a hand covered my mouth. I bit down hard on it and whoever it was let me go. I grabbed a towel and ran back into the room. I snatched the lamp out of the wall, ready to do battle. When the person finally came out of the bathroom, I dropped the lamp. "Abraham?"

"Damn, angel. That hurt! My hand is bleeding."

"Abraham? What are you *doing*? You scared me to death!"

"I was just messing with you," he said with a sneaky look on his face.

"That wasn't funny! You left me here all by myself and then pretended to be a rapist! How was that supposed to be funny?!"

He sat down at the foot of the bed. "Dang, I'm sorry, angel. You got me back, though. You bit the hell out of me."

I rolled my eyes and stepped in front of him. He lifted the towel and wrapped his arms around me. "Where you been?" I asked.

"Taking care of some business. Did you see your food?"

"Yes. Thank you. What business you been taking care of? Why were you gone so long?"

He nodded at a sack sitting on the floor next to the door. "I got some bandages so we can wrap my leg up right and I got us another car. Ditched the other one."

"Oh, okay. How's your leg feel?"

He shrugged. "Okay." He pulled me onto his lap. "You got some fight in you, angel. I like that." He kissed me softly.

"Yeah, well, don't scare me like that again."

He kissed me again. "I won't. I promise. Look, I'm glad you got some fight in you, but I want you to learn how to use this." He reached in his coat pocket and pulled out a gun, a big, heavy-looking gun.

My eyes widened and I stood from his lap. "Is that… is that real?"

"It ain't no toy, that's for sure. I'm gonna teach you how to use it."

I shook my head and backed away from him a little. "I don't wanna know how to use it. I don't wanna shoot anybody."

Abraham stood from the bed, limped closer to me. "Look, angel. There are some bad people out there, people who will try to hurt you for no reason—just because they can. You need to be able to protect yourself, because one day I might not be able to do it."

I frowned. My heart jumped. "What does that mean? Why would you say something like that?! What do you mean?!"

"I don't mean what you think I mean. I mean like, just now, what if it had really been a stranger and not me? You need to be able to protect yourself. That lamp wasn't gonna cut it."

"You shouldn't have left me here like that. That was your fault. You said you'd protect me. You should've been here to protect me. I don't need a gun, I need *you*!" I felt the tears filling my eyes. I didn't want to cry. I was tired of crying. But I couldn't stop myself.

Abraham pulled me to him. "I'm sorry. I'm sorry, angel. I won't do that again. I won't ever leave you like that again. I'm sorry, baby."

I nodded against his chest.

"You forgive me? You know I'd never do anything to hurt you, right. I love you more than anything. I love you more than I love myself, angel."

I looked up at him. "I love you, too."

He smiled down at me. "Good. Come on. I need to get some rest. Been out all day. I'm tired."

"Okay."

After I cleaned Abraham's leg with some soap and water and wrapped it up with the bandages he bought, we climbed into bed and fell asleep in no time.

***

When I woke up, the clock at the bedside said it was 2:00 in the afternoon. We'd turned the heat off and as soon as I peeked from under the covers, I could tell that the room was cool. I threw the covers off of me and climbed out of bed to turn the heater back on. Before I could take one step, I caught a glimpse of something that made me gasp.

The bandages on Abraham's legs were soaked in blood and what looked like pus. The bottom of his leg was darker than the rest of his body. I climbed back into bed and shook him awake. His arm was burning hot when I touched him. He slowly opened his eyes and said, "Huh, angel? What's…" Then he drifted back off to sleep.

I shook him again, harder this time. "Abraham! Wake up!"

This time he not only opened his eyes, but he reached down and grabbed his gun from under the bed and sat up straight. "What is it?! What's going on?! You okay, angel?!"

"It's your leg. Look at it."

He peered down at his leg and shook his head. "We just need to clean it up again, that's all."

I stood from the bed. "No! You have a fever and look at that bandage and your leg is turning darker. I might not be a nurse or a doctor, but I know what an infection looks like. You need help, Abraham. *Medical* help!"

"What am I supposed to do, Meka? I can't go to no hospital. You know that! What you want me to do?!" he said, raising his voice.

"You said you had relatives in Mexico. You said they could help if it was an emergency. *This* is an emergency!"

He sat there and, for a second, I think he thought about going along with me. But then he said, "No, I don't want to bother my uncle with this. I'll be okay."

"How is asking for help bothering him? You said he was like a father to you after your real father died, that he looked out for you and the rest of your family. He'll help you. *Call him*."

"I just don't think it's a good idea to call him, angel."

"Why?"

"I have my reasons."

"None of them are good enough to die over."

"I'm not gonna die."

"Abraham, call him, *please*."

"I… I can't."

I crossed my arms over my bare chest. "Then I ain't having sex with you no more."

He frowned and then he grinned. "You don't really mean that."

"Yes, I do. Wanna try me, Abraham Juan Rios?"

He dropped the grin and gave me a more serious look. "You gotta say my whole name?"

I raised my eyebrows.

"You can't *not* have sex with me, Meka. I'm your husband."

"And I'm your wife and you're supposed to take care of me. How you gonna take care of me if you dead?"

He stared up at me. "You're for real, aren't you?"

"Yep. No doctor, no sex."

"That's wrong, angel. That's real wrong."

I shrugged. "Call your uncle."

"Angel—"

"No sex. I mean it."

He sighed and reached for his cell phone on the bedside table. "Fine. You win."

I smiled. "I knew I would."

8

"MONEY MAKE HER SMILE"

Abraham had only told me two things about his uncle, that he was his late father's only brother and that his name was Juan Carlos Rios. As I sat and listened to Abraham talk to him on the phone, I wondered what about his uncle made him so nervous. I couldn't understand most of what he was saying, but I could tell from the look on his face that he was uncomfortable. After he hung up, he said, "He's sending someone to help." Then he fell back onto the bed and closed his eyes. It almost seemed like that phone call had zapped his energy.

"From where? How long will it take?"

With his eyes still closed, he said, "He knows someone here in Durango. They'll be here in a few minutes. This whole freakin' situation makes me wanna smoke something."

I frowned. "Something like what?"

He opened an eye and looked up at me. "Nothing—never mind. Come lay down with me, angel." He sounded... he sounded *scared*.

I crawled into the bed and he pulled me close to him, held me tighter than he ever had before. I closed my eyes. "You're gonna be okay now. Thank you for calling for help. I don't know what I'd do without you."

He rubbed my back. "I don't know what I'd do without you, either."

I rested my head on his chest and silently prayed that whoever his uncle was sending would really be able to help us. My prayer was interrupted by a knock at the door. We both froze, unsure of who it was. If it was the help his uncle sent, they sure were quick!

I sat up. "I'll get it."

Abraham sprang to his feet, hurt leg and all. "No! I mean, let me get it." He limped to the door. "Who is it?!"

"Juan Carlos sent me," said someone with an American accent.

I stood from the bed and watched as a tall white man walked into the room holding a briefcase. "Are you Abraham?" he asked.

Abraham nodded and glanced at me. "This is my wife."

The man smiled at me. Then he turned back to Abraham. "Well, have a seat and let's have a look."

I watched as he unwrapped Abraham's leg. "Hmm," he said. "Looks like a .38. Good news is it went straight through the muscle, missed the bone. Bad news is it's infected, *badly* infected. Good thing you called your uncle when you did. A little longer and you would've lost your leg."

Abraham looked up at me and shrugged. I gave him a smirk. The doctor, who never told us his name, gave Abraham a shot of antibiotics then he cleaned and wrapped his leg back up. As he was leaving, he said, "I'll be back tomorrow."

Abraham left for the bathroom and stayed in there for so long, I wondered if he got lost or something. When he finally came back out, his eyes were puffy. He climbed into the bed without saying a word to me. I climbed in beside him and he turned his back to me. "Abraham—"

"I'm taking you home."

I frowned. "Home where?"

"Texas. To your aunt's."

I sat up. "What?!"

"This was a mistake. The way we're living, you deserve better, angel. I'm sorry. We should've just waited until you turned 18 to be together."

I stood from the bed. "No! You're not taking me back!"

He rolled over, tears falling from his eyes. "I'm sorry, baby."

"No, Abraham! We're married! You can't take me back!"

"I love you. You'll still be my wife. We'll be together again. Just... just not now."

I felt my own tears begin to flow. "How?! You skipped out on your parole. The police will always be looking for you. How are we going to get back together? How am I gonna live without you? What? You don't want me no more? Is it about the sex? You wanna have sex? We can do it right now."

He sat up and shook his head. "No, Meka. I want you. I'll always love you. It's... I just wanna do what's best for you. What kind of life is this? Always running? Always hiding? You deserve better. That's all I'm saying."

I fell on my knees in tears. "If you take me back, I'll die."

"Come here."

I hung my head. "No."

"Meka, angel... come here."

"No. Just leave me alone!"

I jumped up and ran into the bathroom, shutting and locking the door behind me. I sat on the toilet and cried so hard my head started to hurt. I could hear Abraham knocking on the door and calling my name. I couldn't answer him. It felt like someone took a knife and poked a hole in the middle of my heart over and over again. The thought of losing Abraham hurt worse than the day I had to watch them put my granddaddy in the ground, and I didn't think anything could hurt worse than that. I lowered my head and clutched my hair and screamed.

"Tomeka!" Abraham's voice was louder, so I screamed louder.

More knocking, then beating on the door until finally, it flew open and Abraham rushed into the bathroom and grabbed me. "I'm sorry. I'm sorry. I won't take you back. I'm sorry. I love you. I love you, angel." He kissed me all over my face. "Do you hear me? I love you."

I nodded, buried my head in his chest, and cried some more.

Knock, knock.

Abraham held my face in his hands. "Go get in the bed. I'll get the door."

I nodded, wiped my face, and crawled into bed, pulling the covers over my head. I listened as Abraham answered the door and had a conversation in Spanish. A couple of minutes later, he climbed in bed beside me.

"Who was that?" I asked between sniffles.

"The motel manager. He said someone reported a disturbance. I told him we were okay."

"We got to leave now?"

"We probably should. But not now. Let's just get some rest and we can get something to eat in a little while. I'm sorry, baby. I just want what's best for you. I don't wanna keep putting you in danger."

"*You're* what's best for me."

"Do you... do you miss your family, Meka?"

I shrugged. "Sometimes, but it's okay."

"You happy with me?"

"Yes, very happy. You happy with me?"

"Happier than I've been in my whole life. You've got my heart, angel. My whole heart."

I smiled. "You've got mine, too."

***

Abraham was a little woozy that evening when he left to get us dinner—Subway again. This time, he got us both two foot longs and I'm not ashamed to say that I ate both of mine. We drank our huge cups of soda and after watching a little TV, went to bed.

The doctor arrived bright and early the next morning and when he took the bandages off of Abraham's leg, it looked so much better! I was so relieved; it felt like I'd been holding my breath for days and was finally able to take a breath again. He gave him two shots this time—more antibiotics and another one to numb the leg while he stitched it up. Then he put another bandage on it. He was very nice but not very talkative this time and we still didn't know his name, but I didn't care if it was Crusty the Clown. He'd saved my man and for that, I could've hugged *and* kissed him.

Abraham thanked him. So did I. And as the doctor turned to leave he said, "Your uncle wants you to call him."

I swear Abraham's face turned as white as a sheet of paper. "Um-uh, o-okay. Thank you, again, sir," he stammered.

Then he sat on the side of the bed, holding his cell phone, staring at it. He sat there like that for a couple of minutes.

"Abraham?"

His head snapped in my direction and he just stared at me. I frowned as I sat down beside him. "Abraham? What's wrong?"

He shook his head. "Nothing. Just thinking."

"About what? Taking me back? Please don't start that again."

He reached for my hand. "No. I don't think I could do that even if I really wanted to. I need you, angel. I'd be lost without you."

"Then what is it?"

"I was thinking, when I get well, we should leave Mexico. Go somewhere overseas, maybe. We still got a bunch of money." He looked into my eyes. "Would you wanna do that, angel?"

I shrugged. "I wanna do whatever you wanna do."

He smiled, picked up the phone, and dialed the number. This time, the conversation was in English. "Hello, uncle... yes, he was here... yes, I'm much better, thank you... oh, no, that's not necessary... no, I couldn't... you're too kind... I have a wife, now... meet her?" Then he held the phone tightly and almost squeezed the life out of my hand. "Well, we were planning to leave Mexico, soon... of course I'm grateful... tomorrow?" He looked over at me and dropped his eyes. "Tomorrow is fine. We'll be waiting."

He hung up the phone and with his eyes glued to the floor said, "He wants us to come see him."

"Okay," I said, wondering why he sounded so sad.

He looked up at me. "He's sending someone for us in the morning."

"Sending someone?"

"One of his employees."

"Oh, okay. He's a business man?"

"Yes," Abraham said and then he lay in the bed and didn't say another word to me for the rest of that day. He didn't even protest when I said I was going to get us something to eat. And this time I didn't turn back from Subway. I was kind of tired of eating the same thing but I was also hungry and the hunger won over the boredom. So I got us some sandwiches and chips, stopped at the vending machine for sodas, and went back to my motel home.

***

We lugged our bags out to the waiting car the next morning around 10 AM. The driver placed them in the trunk and then opened the back car door for us. When I climbed inside, my mouth dropped open. It was huge inside with leather seats that reclined just like the nice chairs in Aunt Bobbie's living room. There were *two* TV screens and it smelled so good in there. I knew the car looked shiny and pretty on the outside but I had no idea it would be so fancy on the inside. As I settled into my seat, I said, "Wow! What kind of car is this?"

Abraham climbed in beside me. "I believe it's a Maybach."

My eyes stretched wide. "A Maybach?! Like the rappers talk about in those songs?!"

Abraham nodded.

"Your uncle is rich?!"

"Yes, he is," Abraham said softly.

I looked around, found a remote, and picked it up. I giggled when a movie popped on both screens. There was even a bar. I smiled when Abraham handed me a cold bottle of Coke. *Now this is the life,* I thought.

"Where does he live? Your uncle?"

"You wouldn't know where I was talking about if I told you. It's in the middle of nowhere, really."

Then a thought hit me. "Wait, what if the police have been watching him? I'm sure they know he's your uncle. What if they've been watching him while trying to find us... me?"

Abraham shook his head. "I doubt that. My uncle is very... respected, even by the police. We'll be fine."

"Oh, okay." I turned back to the Brad Pitt movie which had been dubbed in Spanish.

"You like this, Meka? The car, I mean?"

I laughed and nodded. "Yeah! Don't you?"

"It *is* nice. This is the kind of life you deserve. I'ma give it to you one day. I promise."

I looked over at him. "I believe that, but I wouldn't care if we were poor and living in a shack, as long as we're together."

He smiled. "You'll like it at my uncle's place. His wife is American so almost everyone in the house speaks English. He has a daughter who's a little younger than you so you'll have someone to talk to."

I scooted out of my seat and fell into his lap. He laughed. I kissed him and hugged his neck. "I only need to talk to you," I said in his ear.

He looked up at me. "I love you, angel. No matter what happens, don't forget that."

"I love you, too."

***

We rode for hours, stopped for gas, and then rode for more hours. We were in the car for so long that I almost got carsick. Evidently, Abraham was serious about his uncle living in the middle of nowhere. I was afraid that if the driver drove us any further, he'd drive us right off the planet. We rode through miles and miles of nothing but desert and mountains, blue skies and highways. We rode for hours without passing by a single house or animal. The highway was empty as well. We hadn't passed by another car in a very long time.

I was tired but also excited and kind of scared. That was probably because of Abraham. He'd been quiet for most of the ride except for a few sighs. And when he wasn't sighing, he was tapping his foot or cracking his knuckles. And if he wasn't doing that, he was staring out the window with this weird look on his face. He didn't say a word to me or even turn and look at me for a good while.

Finally, out in the middle of nowhere, we approached a high stone wall that surrounded something. It reminded me of those walls that surrounded the cities in those Bible movies my granny used to watch on TV all the time, except there was barbed wire at the top of these walls. The driver stopped at a gate, rolled down his window, and punched in a code. I stared at the numbers as he pressed the buttons, *one-five-two-three*. The huge metal gates slowly opened and the car rolled through them.

My mouth dropped open when I saw the huge house that stood inside of those walls. It was incredible! My aunt's house in Houston was big. She had four bedrooms and three bathrooms. She even had a guest house and a pool. But this house was ten times as big as my Aunt Bobbie Ann's, maybe even more than that. The house was light beige stucco with a tiled roof—what the folks on the HGTV channel I used to watch with Aunt Bobbie Ann would call Spanish style. It was beautiful and looked more like a palace than a house. The driveway made a circle around a huge fountain that stood right in front of the house. There was a stable and horses to one side, a smaller house that looked just like the big house to the other side. There was a five-car garage attached to the house. Five cars?! Yeah, this guy had mucho dinero.

I sat there and stared up at the huge house and caught a glimpse of a young girl standing in a window upstairs. I figured she must've been the cousin Abraham told me about. The driver pulled to a stop right in front of the steps that led up to the front door. The front door opened and a young guy dressed in a black suit came out and opened the car door for us as the driver got our bags from the trunk. As we climbed out of the car, I noticed two big lion statues sitting on each side of the steps. Abraham grabbed my hand, squeezed it, and kissed my cheek before leading me up the steps and into the house. There, in the huge foyer, we were met by a short man with darkly tanned skin and thinning black hair with several strands of gray peeking through. He wore a white suit, lots of gold necklaces and rings, and a beige smile. The diamonds on his huge watch glistened as he raised his arms and hugged Abraham tightly.

"¡El sobrino! Nephew! Ha!" He nearly shouted with an accent so thick, I could barely understand him. Then he turned to me and smiled. He reached for my hand, squeezed it, and then softly kissed it. He looked up at Abraham. "Jor wife?"

Abraham nodded. "Tomeka, this is my uncle, Juan. Uncle, this is my wife, my angel, Tomeka."

He looked me up and down and smiled. "Ah, beautiful, absolutely beautiful, *hermosa*. Truly an angel. Ju did well, nephew. Terri!" he shouted. "Come see Abraham and hees wife!"

A few seconds later, a tall, gorgeous, dark-skinned black woman entered the foyer wearing a flowing, multicolored dress. She smiled as Uncle Juan pulled her close to his side. She was at least two inches taller and twenty years younger than him. He kissed her cheek and said, "Tomeka, dees is my wife, Terri."

"Well, hello," she said with a refined American accent. "Welcome to our home. We call it 'The Den.'"

I smiled and said, "Mucho gusto." *Well,* I thought, *like uncle, like nephew.*

PART
TWO:
THE DEN

(Tomeka)

9

"SWIMMING POOLS"

Our guest bedroom in Uncle Juan's house was huge. I think it was almost as big as my granny's entire house! There was an enormous bed on a platform with a pretty gold comforter and tons of pillows piled on it. There was a gigantic window with a view of the backyard, and beyond the yard you could see snow-capped mountains in the distance. But that backyard was something else! There was a big pool, a tennis court, a gazebo, and what seemed like miles and miles of green grass. I wondered how they kept that grass so green way out in the desert.

There was a sitting area with a couch and a fireplace in our room, and we even had our own bathroom. This place was like Heaven! I walked over to the bed, flopped down on my back, closed my eyes, and smiled. "This room is incredible, Abraham!"

Abraham sat down next to me and laid his hand on my thigh. "You like this, huh?"

I nodded. "Of course! Who wouldn't? Don't you?"

"Yeah... it's nice."

I sat up and looked at him. "Nice?! This is the *bomb*, Abraham! It's the business, for real!"

"Yeah, I know, angel," he said softly. He almost sounded sad.

I climbed into his lap and faced him. "What's wrong?"

He shrugged. "Tired, I guess. That was a long ride, cielito."

I kissed him. "I know. Wanna take a nap?"

He smiled. "Only if you take it with me."

I gave him a sly look. "Or we could do something else. I think I owe you since you called your uncle like I asked."

His smile widened. "Oh, yeah?"

"Yeah..."

He rubbed his hand up and down my back. "You know you don't even have to ask if I wanna do that. I *always* wanna do that."

I hugged him and whispered. "Go lock the door."

He grinned. "Yes, ma'am."

Before either of us could move a muscle, there was a knock at the door, and then it flew open. It scared me so bad, I jumped up from Abraham's lap. He jumped up, too.

"Cousin!" The girl from the window shrieked as she ran into the room and hugged Abraham. She was short and kind of chubby with long, dark brown hair and a really pretty round face. She looked nothing like Abraham's Aunt Terri.

"Ha! You're all grown up, now!" Abraham said as he hugged her back. Once she finally let him go, he said, "Trinity, this is my wife, Meka. Meka, this is my beautiful cousin, Trinity. I used to call her little Trinity, but I can't anymore."

Trinity giggled. I held out my hand and she grabbed it and pulled me into a hug. "You're family!" she exclaimed in my ear. "No handshakes for family!"

I smiled. She seemed so sweet, and she was so excited about seeing Abraham.

"I'm so glad you guys are here! It gets lonely here now that JC is gone to college," she said as she sat down at the foot of the bed.

Abraham looked at me. "JC's my other little cousin, Trinity's brother. He's in California, right? In college?"

She nodded. "Yup! It's just me and Mommy and Papi here. Oh, and the bodyguards, too. As soon as I turned sixteen, Papi got me my own bodyguard. He is soooo overprotective." She rolled her eyes.

Abraham reached for my hand and held onto it. "You're his little girl," he said. "I'm sure I'll be the same way when me and Meka have a little girl."

Trinity's eyes widened. "Are you pregnant?!"

I frowned a little and shook my head. "Oh, no."

Abraham wrapped his arm around my shoulders. *"Not yet."*

"You guys look so in love! I can't wait until I get married and have kids!"

I smiled up at Abraham. "Yeah, it's great."

A man peeked into the room at us.

"Oh, this is Cesar, my bodyguard." She lowered her voice. "See. Like I said, *overprotective.*"

I waved at Cesar and he ducked back out of the doorway.

"Well, I'll leave you guys alone now. See you at dinner!" And with that, she flounced out of the room, closing the door behind her.

"She's nice but she doesn't look like her mother or her father," I said.

"Terri's not her mom. Her mom died when she was little but she looks just like her."

"Oh, that's sad," I said softly, thinking about my own mother.

Abraham pulled me close to him and tilted his head to the side. "Hey, you okay?"

I nodded. "Yeah, I'm fine. Just thinking about stuff that doesn't matter."

"Well, why don't I give you something else to think about," he said with a grin.

"Like what?"

"Like where were we before Trinity came in here?"

I grinned as I reached up and kissed him. "In the bed. Hey, is your uncle the reason you like black girls?"

He looked a little surprised. "What makes you think I like black girls?"

"You like me, don't you?"

His eyes widened. "You're black?"

I rolled my eyes. "Stop playing, Abraham."

"I guess he influenced my taste a little, but you got one thing wrong," he said and then buried his face in my neck.

"What?"

"I don't like you… I *love* you."

"I love you, too."

He let go of me and then fell onto the bed. "Then come over here and show me you love me."

I smiled as I climbed into the bed with him.

***

We had dinner in the big dining room on expensive-looking dishes while sitting in expensive-looking chairs. The food was so good, I had to slow down because I was eating way too fast. All we'd had to eat before we got to Uncle Juan's house was Subway and vending machine food. Even back in our place in Mexico City, we *never* ate like this!

We had tacos arabes, tamales y pozole, and enchiladas verdes. I drank so much watermelon agua fresca, I thought my bladder would explode, and for dessert, we had churros with chocolate sauce. Uncle Juan said that the dinner was a celebration of our arrival. I caught him looking at me once or twice, but I think he was just happy to see us—happy we were there. I was happy to be there, too.

After dinner, he led us to his theater. Yes, he had an actual theater in his house and he had all of the new movies that were still in the theaters! We watched the new Kevin Hart movie and I laughed so hard my stomach hurt. But a few times when I looked over at Abraham, he was looking so serious, almost with a frown on his face. I reached for his hand and squeezed it and smiled at him. He smiled back at me, but I could tell something was wrong.

When we finally went to bed, I asked, "Are you okay?"

He pulled me close to him. "I'm fine, angel."

"You sure?"

"Yeah, I'm good. Just tired from the ride and the excitement. Just ready to get this leg better so we can move on, you know?"

"Okay."

"I love you, Meka. I really do. You know that, right?"

I looked up at him in the darkness. "I know. I love you, too. You know *that*, right?"

"I knew that when you left your aunt's house that night to be with me. Thank you. Thank you for loving me enough to do that, cielito. I promise I'm gonna make things good for us."

"Things are good, Abraham. They're great."

"I'm glad you think so, angel."

I closed my eyes and soon drifted off to sleep, but I woke up in the middle of the night to use the bathroom. All of that food seemed to run right through me. When I climbed back into the bed, I couldn't shake a feeling that I'd had ever since I woke up. It felt like someone was watching us.

10

"LOST IN PARADISE"

When I woke up the next morning, Abraham was already out of the bed. I looked around and didn't find him anywhere in the bedroom or the bathroom. I shrugged and decided that maybe he was already eating breakfast or maybe the doctor was there to see him. I took a shower and dressed and then made up the bed. I looked around the room and, for the first time, noticed a desk with a laptop computer sitting on it.

I hadn't used a computer since before I left my Aunt Bobbie Ann's house. Before then, I only got to use the computer at school since Granny wouldn't allow us to have one at her house. I sat down at the desk and lifted the top of the computer then hit the power button. I watched the screen light up and was relieved to see that there was no password required to log on. In two seconds, I was on the internet. I took a deep breath and then typed in my name— Tomeka Sharnay Brooks.

The first thing that popped up was a website labeled, "Help Us Find Tomeka." I clicked on it and my eyes stretched wide at the page full of pictures of me—some with Sharee and some by myself. There was even a video. I clicked on the little icon to play the video and watched as Aunt Bobbie Ann's face appeared before me.

"Tomeka left my house in the middle of the night in early June of this year and has not been seen since. We know that she is with a young man whose name is Abraham Rios. We are almost certain that he has taken Tomeka out of the country as he has family in Mexico who might be helping him. He is a convicted felon who has violated his parole. He is also an adult. Tomeka is a minor. As you can see from the picture on my t-shirt, Tomeka is dark brown-skinned with black, shoulder-length hair and brown eyes. She is about 5'7" tall with a slim build. Abraham is Hispanic, 5'9" tall, with dark hair and a medium build. We are asking that anyone who even thinks they've seen Tomeka contacts the authorities, or you can call our tip line at 555-555-3211. Tomeka, if you are watching this, know that we love you and we miss you so much." She paused as her voice trembled. She wiped a tear from her cheek. "We miss you and your granny is so worried. Come home, sweetie. No questions asked. No one is mad at you. We just want you to come home."

I paused the video and laid my head on the desk. My eyes were filled with tears but my head was filled with questions. I never meant to hurt anyone, I just wanted to be with Abraham, and if I'd stayed with my family, that never would've happened. They wouldn't have let it happen because of my age and his past. But I loved him. So wasn't leaving with him the right thing to do? If I hadn't then I would've been miserable, and I would've made everyone around me miserable. And I just didn't believe that my granny was worried about me. Not really. As a matter of fact, I was sure she was probably relieved I was gone.

I lifted my head and resumed the video. I watched as Sharee's face appeared on the screen. She looked so... so sad. And as soon as she started to talk, she began to cry. So did I. "Tomeka, I wish you would just come back home. I... I miss you. I think about you all the time. I hope you'll call or something and let us know you're okay." Then she broke down. The screen went blank and then the hotline number popped up on the screen.

I closed the laptop and then walked over to the bed and lay on my face. I cried so hard that my head started to hurt. My heart hurt so badly. The look on Sharee's face and the sound of her voice, her tears—it was all too much for me. I lay there for a long time, because I just didn't have the strength to get up. I wanted to call them just so they would know that I was okay, but I knew I couldn't do that. I knew that was too risky and no matter how bad I felt about hurting my family, I'd never risk getting Abraham arrested. Because I still loved him more than anything or anyone in the world.

I rolled over on my back and stared at the ceiling. Maybe I could use my burner phone and then get rid of it. Just one phone call, that's all I'd need to make. I just needed for them to know that I was okay. Just one call. That's it. As soon as I got up the nerve, I'd ask Abraham. He'd understand. Surely he would.

I sat up straight in the bed when I heard the knock at the door. Then I just stared at it. After a minute I walked over to it and said, "Who is it?"

"Trinity."

I wiped my face and opened the door. Abraham's cousin walked in with a smile on her face. "Buenos dias," she chirped.

"Buenos dias."

"Abraham wanted me to tell you that he'll be back in a little while."

"Oh, where is he?"

"Somewhere with my papa. Are you hungry? There's plenty of food. I was just going down to eat. Then I have school." She didn't sound too happy about school. For some reason, I actually missed school a little bit.

"Okay." I followed her out of the room and was startled when I saw her bodyguard standing outside the door.

Trinity giggled. "Oh, this is Cesar, my bodyguard. Remember him?"

I nodded. "Um, hi."

"I know it's weird, but Papa insists that he follow me everywhere I go, *all the time*."

I frowned slightly. "Even in the house?"

She nodded. "Yep. Talk about *overkill*. Geez."

I smiled as I followed her down the stairs and into the dining room. "Why do you guys call this house 'The Den?'" I asked.

She shrugged. "Who knows? My parents are weird."

I nodded and thought, *can't be as weird as mine.*

The table was again filled with food. And my eyes were again bigger than my stomach. I ate way too much but I just couldn't stop myself.

Afterwards, Trinity said, "You wanna go to school with me?"

"I should wait here for Abraham, I think. Besides, will they let me go with you? I mean, the teachers?"

"Sure. I go to school downstairs, in the study. I'm homeschooled."

"Oh. Okay, then."

I sat in a corner of the study while an older, white lady taught Trinity, who was the exact same age as me—16—all about literature. Sitting there listening to them, I decided that I didn't miss school after all. My mind began to drift back to what I'd seen on the computer, to my aunt's and sister's faces. To how sad and worried they looked. And I felt sad and worried, too. I'd never really considered that they'd be so worried, but I guess to them I'd disappeared without a trace.

I looked around the room at the tall bookcases that were built into the walls and were full of books and at the beautiful furniture that was crowded into the room. Every room in that huge house was lovely. It felt like a big museum. The furniture was so nice I hated to sit on it.

I looked around some more and noticed Cesar sitting in an opposite corner from me. Why in the world would Trinity need a body guard at all times? Talk about strange.

About an hour later, I excused myself from "school" and headed back up to my room to lie down. All that boring literature talk had made me sleepy. On the way, I ran into Uncle Juan Carlos. He stopped me on the staircase.

"Ju looking for some-ting?" he asked as his eyes took me in from head to toe. It was like he was hungry and I was a pork chop or a chicken leg or something. The way he looked at me made my skin crawl.

"Uh… no, I was just going back to my room. Is… is Abraham back, too?"

"No, he still had some… business to take care of."

"Oh, okay."

"He be back soon." He smiled and licked his lips. "Ju need any-ting, any-ting at all, while he gone, ju jus' let me know, eh?"

I gave him a nervous smile. "O… okay. Thanks-gracias."

"De nada, beautiful."

I nearly ran the rest of the way to my room. I shut the door behind me and climbed into bed and despite the creepiness of my encounter with Uncle Juan, I fell right to sleep.

I'd only been asleep for a little while when the sound of someone gagging and grunting and... *whimpering* woke me up. I sat up in the huge bed and tried to figure out where the sound was coming from. Then I heard it again. I slowly walked to the bathroom and tapped on the closed door. More grunting. "Abraham, is that you? Are you okay?"

"Uh, I'll be out in a minute, angel."

I pressed my ear to the door. "Abraham, what's wrong?"

"Nothing, baby! Just… just give me a minute!" he shouted.

I backed away from the door all the way to the bed and sat down. I stared at the door, listened to him gag and grunt. Was he sick? After several minutes of waiting, he finally walked out of the bathroom. His eyes were puffy and he looked pale. He climbed into the bed without saying a word to me.

"Were you throwing up? Are you sick?"

He turned his back to me. "I'm okay."

"You sure? Want me to get you something for your stomach? I bet they have something around here."

"No, angel. Just come here." He lifted his arm and, as soon as I lay down beside him, wrapped it around me. He didn't say another word. Neither did I. We just lay there for the rest of the day.

For the next three days, there was more of the same. Abraham would be gone when I woke up in the morning. I would go to breakfast and school with Trinity and her bodyguard and then to our room for a nap. Abraham would return, pale-faced and sick. But he wouldn't talk. On the third day, he refused to go downstairs for dinner. He had me bring his food to our room. When I asked him what was going on, he wouldn't answer or he'd lie and say "nothing."

I was so worried about him, but more than that, I needed to talk to him. While he was gone every day, I'd been checking that website, watching that video over and over again and my heart was so heavy. I wanted to call home badly. I really needed to talk to him about that, but I couldn't even get him to say "hi" or "bye," let alone have a full conversation.

Finally, the disappearing for most of the day stopped and Abraham started to act more like himself again. The doctor had been seeing him every night and he said that his leg was much better. We'd been staying at his uncle's for little over a week and things were finally beginning to feel normal between us again.

We were still in bed together, early one morning before the sun had risen, when I asked the question. "Can I use one of the burner phones to call home?"

Abraham didn't answer but I knew he was awake.

"Um, I know they're worried about me," I continued. "I just wanna call so they'll know I'm okay. That's all."

Abraham sat up and turned a lamp on. "You want to go back?"

"No! I just... I know they're worried about me, my sister especially. I just want to call and let them know I'm okay. That's it. One call. I'll make it really quick."

He stared at me for a moment, and then he said, "Okay. You can use mine. I'll ditch it when you're done."

He handed me the phone and I just held it for a minute or so. Then I dialed my aunt's number. I was sure there was some time difference but I wasn't sure by how much time since I didn't know exactly where in Mexico Uncle Juan's house was located. I closed my eyes as the phone rang in my ear and hoped someone was there to answer. Then I heard a soft, "Hello?" It was my Aunt Bobbie Ann.

My eyes filled with tears. "Hello, Aunt Bobbie Ann? It's... it's Tomeka."

"Tomeka! Tomeka, where are you?!"

"I... I just wanted you and everybody to know that I'm okay. Don't worry about me, I'm doing fine."

"Tomeka... listen, sweetie, where are you? I'll come get you no matter how far away you are. *Where are you?*"

I looked over at Abraham as I wiped the tears from my eyes. "I gotta go now. Tell everyone I'm okay. I love you all." I hung up and fell against Abraham and cried.

***

It was hard for me after that—hard to be happy, hard not to think about my family. I tried to act like I had before, like I didn't care about being away from them, but I don't know if Abraham believed me. Plus, I kept having that weird feeling that I was being watched.

We'd been there at Uncle Juan's house for weeks. I liked sleeping in that beautiful room and eating all of that good food and there seemed to be a party full of food, beer, and music every other night.

It reminded me of back when my dad was dating Dee. I loved being with him back then. But of course he screwed that up like he did everything else.

Anyway, Trinity was nice, and I liked talking to her. It was great being around her since we were the same age. I liked everyone, really, but as much fun as we were having at Uncle Juan's and as nice as everyone was to us, a part of me would be glad when we left. Talking to my aunt had changed my thinking. For the first time since I left, I started to think that running away with Abraham may have been a bad idea.

While Abraham was downstairs talking to his uncle one day, I did something that I used to see my granny do all the time. I got down on my knees and I prayed for God to help me. I prayed that he would comfort my family. I prayed for Him to show me what to do. I prayed for a long, long time. Just as I was getting to my feet, there was a knock at the door. I knew it was Trinity before I even opened it, but instead of the smile she usually wore, there were tears rolling down her cheeks as she walked into the room and stood in front of the window.

"Um, Trinity? What's wrong?"

She placed a finger to her mouth and said, "Shh." Then she beckoned for me to come to her.

I frowned and wondered what was going on. "What?" I asked as I walked over to her.

"Keep your voice down," she whispered.

I turned and looked at the closed door then back at her. "What is going on?" I asked softly.

"He can hear you. He can hear and see *everything*. That's how he knew. It has to be."

"Who? What are you talking about?" All of the whispering was just weird.

"My papa. *He knows.*"

"He knows what?"

"About me and Cesar, my bodyguard. We're in love just like you and Abraham. We were trying to keep it a secret, but he found out. He must've seen us somehow."

Huh? "Seen you what?"

"Having sex."

"What?!" I shrieked and then lowered my voice again to match hers. "How do you know he knows?"

"Because I have a new bodyguard and when I asked my papa where Cesar was, he said he'd had an accident and wouldn't be coming back. There's no way Cesar wouldn't say goodbye to me. He loved me. Oh, God, I hope my papa didn't kill him."

"*Kill him?* Why would he kill him? For… for what he did with you?"

She rolled her eyes as the tears continued to fall. "Because that's what he does. He *kills* people."

I frowned. "I don't understand."

"He's a horrible man. He watches everything, he knows everything, and no one is safe around him—not me and especially not you. He likes young girls, you know. He destroys everything and everyone. He thinks he's the king of everything. Even the police are afraid of him. That's why they call this place 'The Den.' Because he calls himself el león—the lion. I *hate* him."

A knock at the door almost made me scream. Trinity and I both jumped. I stood there and stared at the door, afraid to move an inch. Trinity didn't move, either. We stood there next to each other, her face wet with tears, mine covered with fear. Then came another knock and the door swung open. Trinity's mother walked into the room and tried to smile at me but even though her mouth was forming her smile, the rest of her face, even the way she walked into the room, told me that the smile wasn't real. She looked just as scared as I felt.

"Trinity, it's time for your dance lesson. Did you forget? Señora Sonia is waiting."

Trinity wiped her face and shook her head. "I don't wanna dance today."

Terri glanced at me. "Trinity, if you know what's good for you, you'll come with me *right now*."

"Where's Cesar? Is he dead? Did Papa kill him?"

Terri grabbed Trinity's arm. "What is wrong with you, saying something like that?" she asked in a harsh whisper. "You are going to get yourself down stairs and dance right now!" She tugged on her arm. As she pulled her past me, Trinity looked at me and mouthed, "Watch out. He's watching you." Then Terri pulled her out of the room.

I walked over to the bed, sat down, and looked around. I wondered if what Trinity had said was true. Was there a camera somewhere in the room? Was that why I always felt like someone was watching me? If it was true, they'd gotten an eyeful of me and Abraham in that bed. I shook my head. "She's just upset. She didn't really mean it," I whispered to myself. But still, I couldn't stand the thought of sitting there in that room alone anymore. So I left and walked downstairs.

I found Abraham and his uncle along with some other men sitting in the study, talking. His uncle looked up at me and winked and I felt a chill run down my spine. I backed away from the room and continued to walk through the house towards the piano music that I could faintly hear. I walked past room after room. It felt like there was no end to that house. It was so big that it almost felt like a city instead of a house.

I was getting closer to the music when I noticed a door, the only closed door I'd seen on the first floor. Something about it caught my attention. It looked the same as all of the other doors. I didn't hear any strange noise. I really don't know what drew me to that door other than the fact that it was closed.

I walked over to it and tried the knob. It was locked. I looked around to be sure no one was watching me and then I pressed my ear to the door and closed my eyes. I strained my ears, trying to hear something, anything. I stood there for an entire minute before deciding that I was crazy. It was probably just a closet. What was I expecting to hear? Just as I was backing away from the door, I heard it. A whimper. A faint whimper. It sounded like a girl or a woman. I pressed my ear to the door again and whispered, "Hello? Is someone in there?"

Silence.

"Hello?" I whispered again.

"What are you doing?"

I jumped and my heart felt like it was about to hop out of my chest as I turned to face Abraham. I fell against him, relieved it was him and not someone else. "I thought I heard someone in that room. Do you know what that room is?"

"No, but it's not a good idea to be snooping around here. What were you looking for?"

"Um… I was looking for Trinity. I wanted to watch her dance."

"Well, I need to talk to you. Take a walk with me instead." He looked so serious.

I nodded. "Okay."

We walked out the back door into the huge back yard. We walked and walked until I started wondering if we were leaving the property altogether. When Abraham finally stopped, we were just inches from the wall that surrounded Uncle Juan's home. He held my face gently in his hands. "If I tell you something, can you keep your cool?"

"What do you mean? Keep my cool?"

He darted his eyes around us. "I need to tell you something. I need to get something off my chest, but I need for you to stay calm until we can leave here."

I nodded slowly. "Okay…"

He slid to the ground and took a seat on a mound of what I now realized was fake grass. I sat down beside him. He let out a breath and looked up at me with fear in his eyes. He took my hand and squeezed it. When he finally spoke, his voice was so soft, I barely heard him. "Remember when we first got here, all those days I left early and got back late?"

I nodded.

"Uncle Juan took me back to Guadalajara to find the guys who attacked me and shot me."

My eyes widened.

He continued. "We found them. All three of them. And uh, he

made me... we tied them up out in the desert. Then we... we tortured them—cut them, stabbed them, did all sorts of crazy stuff to them that I don't even want to think about, let alone talk about. *Sick stuff.* They begged us to stop. They cried. Ain't nothing like seeing a grown man cry, you know? That's some sad stuff. One of 'em even prayed to die, begged me to kill them, but my uncle said to let them suffer, that killing them would be too good for them. They're still tied up out there. Probably dead by now. Animals have probably gotten to them. I was mad about getting shot, but that stuff Juan Carlos made me do? I don't think they deserved that. He's ... he's crazy. He's *always* been crazy."

"Oh, wow, Abraham. I'm so sorry. That must've been horrible for you. Makes my stomach ache just hearing about it. That's why you didn't wanna call him, isn't it? Because he's... crazy?"

He nodded. "That's part of the reason. I knew he was dangerous. He's into all kinds of illegal stuff. Got the cops on his payroll. I just didn't wanna get mixed up in his world again."

"Dangerous to us?"

Abraham shook his head. "No... I don't know. He's the reason I went to jail. I was working for him when I got caught selling drugs. He, um, wants me to work for him again."

"You're not going to, are you?! You said you were never gonna do that again!"

He reached for my hand. "My uncle is not the kind of man you say no to, angel. Plus, I owe him for getting me well again. I have to do it, but it'll only be for a little while and then we can leave here. One good thing is we'll have even more money to take with us. We can go anywhere we want."

"So, you're gonna do it?"

He nodded. "I really don't have a choice. I'll be gone for a few days. Just keep to yourself and don't go snooping around. Understand?"

I dropped my eyes. "I don't want you to go. Why can't I just go with you?"

"Because this is business, angel. I can't do my job if you're with me. My mind won't be clear. And it's just too dangerous."

I sighed. "But…" I paused and lowered my voice. "Abraham, Trinity said something earlier. She was really upset and she said some stuff that scared me."

"What? What'd she say?"

"She was mad at your uncle about her boyfriend and she said that your uncle watches everything that goes on in the house. That he knows everything. It's true, isn't it? That's why you brought me way out here to talk?"

"I wouldn't put it past him. He's controlling, thinks he owns the world. This whole family is a little… different. Look, just be careful. Keep doing what you've been doing and you'll be fine."

I frowned. "But Abraham, if he watches everything, that means he's seen us… *you know*."

Abraham smiled a little. "Well, we were just doing what married people do. I don't care who watches."

"Well, I do. It's creepy for an old man to watch us like that. I can't do it anymore in that house. I can't wait until we get out of here. And…"

"And what? What is it, angel?"

"And… don't leave."

He pulled me close to him and kissed me. "It'll be okay. I'll only be gone for three, four days, tops. Just hang tight. We'll be leaving here soon."

"Abraham, I don't want you to leave me. I'm really scared, like *for real*."

Abraham pulled away from me and looked me in the eye. "Did Trinity say something else that scared you?"

I nodded.

He rubbed my cheek with his hand. "What was it, cielito?"

"Is… is your uncle going with you?"

He frowned. "No, just me and some of the other guys who work for him. Why? What did Trinity say?"

I sucked in a breath and blew it out. "She said that he's been watching me because he likes young girls. I kind of believe her. He creeps me out with the way he looks at me sometimes. What if he tries to do something to me?"

He shook his head and gave me a little smile. "She was just mad. My uncle respects family. He wouldn't touch you. I'm sure of that. In some ways, he's the most normal person in that house when it comes to family."

"What do you mean?"

"Never mind. Look, everything will be fine. You know I wouldn't let anything happen to you, angel."

I looked up at him. "Promise?"

"Promise."

11

"HUNTER"

The first night I had to spend alone in Uncle Juan's house, I couldn't sleep at all. I lay awake in bed for most of the night, and around 2:00 A.M., I got up and logged onto the computer. I checked the website and watched the video of my aunt and sister again. Then I surfed the news website and read some of the headlines—a wildfire in California, a kidnapping in Denver, a missing girl in Mexico. The last headline, dated over a month earlier, caught my interest. I clicked on the link and my eyes raced across the screen, reading the words.

The girl had been found in an apartment in Mexico City, severely malnourished and nearly dead from exposure. Her brother, who was also found with her, was already dead when the authorities arrived. The girl was rushed to a local hospital and was eventually discharged to the home of a relative since the authorities were unable to locate her parents. The girl was sitting outside of the relative's house when a man drove up and forced her to leave with him. The article said she'd been missing ever since. As I scrolled to the bottom of the page, my eyes widened and I gasped. The girl in the picture was my friend, Maribel.

I sat there and stared at the picture. Not many days passed that I didn't wonder what happened to her, and I was glad she'd been taken to the hospital and eventually left healthy. But she'd been kidnapped? How much bad stuff could happen to one person? I closed my eyes and prayed for her. I hoped they'd find her and that she would be safe.

I opened my eyes and felt a chill run down my spine. I felt that feeling again—like someone was watching me. But this time, the feeling was much stronger. I could almost feel someone breathing on the back of my neck. In my soul, I knew someone was in that room with me. I *felt* it.

I pressed the button to turn the computer off. After the screen went black, I sat and stared at it—afraid to move but also afraid to keep sitting there. I decided that I'd go downstairs and fix myself a snack and maybe the eerie feeling would be gone when I got back. As I turned my head, I caught a glimpse of a reflection on the computer screen. It was the outline of a figure—a person.

I jumped up from the chair and spun around. I peered into the darkness. "Who's there?"

Silence.

My heart slammed against my ribcage. "Who's there? Un-Uncle Juan?"

I heard something. A footstep?

I backed against the desk, almost knocking it over. "Please tell me who you are. What do you want?"

The bedroom door slowly opened and the person left. There was no light on in the hallway, so I still couldn't make out the figure as they left the room. After they closed the door, I rushed to it and locked it. Then I told myself that whoever had been in the room probably had a key. So I pushed the heavy chest of drawers against the door and then sat on the side of the bed and cried.

***

I woke up late the next morning, sitting on the floor with my back against the chest of drawers which was still blocking the door. I glanced around the room and saw that I was still alone. I knew the door was blocked but I was still afraid that someone was in the room watching me. There could've been a secret door or something for all I knew. I was very hungry but more than that, I was scared—too scared to move the chest of drawers or to leave the room. I wanted to take a shower but I was too scared to do that, too. So I just sat there and stared and tried not to cry. I missed Abraham terribly, and I wished he was there with me. I wished he was there to protect me. I wished I could leave and never come back. I looked over at the computer on the desk and wondered about my family. It would be better to be with them than to be alone and afraid. *Anything* would be better than this.

I finally got up the nerve to take a shower about an hour later. By then, I was starving and my hunger trumped my fear. So after I got dressed, I headed downstairs around what would've been lunchtime in America but was still considered breakfast in Mexico. I was relieved to find that I was the only person in the dining room. I had no idea where Uncle Juan or Trinity or Aunt Terri or any of their ten or twenty bodyguards were and I didn't care. I hoped I could eat fast enough to avoid them all.

No such luck. I was so hungry that I ended up eating quite a bit, taking second helpings of everything in front of me. I was just about done when Terri joined me at the table.

She smiled as she sat down across from me and draped a napkin across her lap. "Buenos dias," she said. She really was a beautiful woman. I wondered why she was with Juan Carlos. Then I remembered he was rich.

I looked up at her and tried to smile. "Buenos dias."

"This food looks so good and I'm starving. So you're eating breakfast a little later, too, eh?"

I dropped my eyes back to my plate. "Yes, I... I woke up late." I couldn't exactly tell her that I thought her husband was in my room watching me last night so I didn't get much sleep.

"Hmm, missing Abraham?"

I looked up at her and nodded. "Yes, I miss him a lot."

"I bet you do. Young love is wonderful. I remember when Juan Carlos and I first fell in love. That was a long time ago. Trinity and CJ were just little kids. Their mother had just died."

I smiled and then I wondered if a smile was really appropriate.

"Got any plans for today?" she asked.

I frowned slightly. What plans could I possibly have with Abraham gone? "No, ma'am. I mean, I guess I could go to school with Trinity for the rest of the day."

She shook her head, swallowed a forkful of food, and said, "Oh, Trinity's not here, sweetie. She's off at boarding school."

I laid my fork down. "Boarding school? She didn't mention anything about boarding school the last time I talked to her."

She sipped some water and nodded. "Well, she didn't know about it. Juan Carlos and I decided it would be best for her."

"Oh." I wondered if her being sent away had anything to do with her bodyguard. I also wondered if he was dead.

She laughed lightly. "You know what? Juan is under the impression that after Trinity saw you and Abraham, she got it in her head that she could be with her bodyguard."

"Oh, well, I—"

"Of course I told him that was nonsense. You're of age, right? After all, you and Abraham are married."

Something about her—her voice and the way she was looking at me—made me very uncomfortable. "Uh, yes, ma'am," I said.

"Good. Some of the men around here are known to take advantage of young, underage girls. That's one of the reasons we sent Trinity away." She paused and looked at me for a moment. "Do you think you could help me with something after you've finished eating?"

I nodded, though I wanted to lie and say no, but how could I when I was living in her house and had no way of leaving? "Sure. I'm done now."

"Okay. Go on up to your room. I'll come and get you."

***

I waited upstairs in my room for an hour. Aunt Terri hadn't showed up and I hated having to wait in that room. Since that room creeped me out and I knew someone was basically stalking me, I wasn't looking forward to spending another night in there alone, either. I knew I wouldn't get a wink of sleep that night. I walked over to the big window and looked out at the back yard. It was amazing that I could feel so miserable in such a beautiful place, that this big house could feel like such a prison. I sighed and decided to head back downstairs and try to find Aunt Terri. I couldn't stay in that room another second.

I walked downstairs and checked the dining room. The table had been cleared and there was no sign of Aunt Terri. There was no one in the kitchen except for the cook and one of the maids. I found the room where Trinity went to school empty. I continued through the house, moving from empty room to empty room. In fact, the entire first floor was eerily quiet and deserted.

I was heading back toward the staircase, on my way to see if Aunt Terri was upstairs somewhere, when I passed the door again—the mysterious closed door. I stood there in the middle of the hall and stared at that door for a good while. I checked the hallway, strained my ears, but I saw and heard nothing. As a matter of fact, the silence scared me more than if someone had been standing right behind me, watching my every move. I thought about Abraham's warning. *"Just keep to yourself and don't go snooping around. Understand?"*

But in my mind, this was not snooping. I was just looking for Aunt Terri. I lightly knocked on the door and whispered, "Is anyone in there? Aunt Terri?"

Silence.

I stood there for another minute and then told myself that I was being silly. It was probably just a closet. I stared at the knob. I wanted to try it, to see if it was still locked, but I was afraid to touch it. What if it *was* locked? What if it *wasn't*?

I reached for the knob, slowly placed my hand on it, and began to twist it. My eyes widened as I realized that it wasn't locked. I slowly opened the door to find that it wasn't a closet after all. It was a room—a bedroom. I sighed with relief and then wondered what I had expected to find behind the door? A dead body? I shook my head as I turned to leave and then I stopped. *It won't hurt to look around*, I thought.

My eyes searched the room—pretty twin bed with white comforter, small desk, dresser with mirror. It looked like a girl's room. There were lots of bottles of perfume on the dresser and near the window, there was a rack with a bunch of dresses hanging on it—beautiful dresses. Then I saw it—another door. I walked over to it and tried the knob only to find that it was locked. I frowned slightly and then for some reason, I decided to knock on it. But as soon as I did, I shook my head. I was sure it was just a closet. What kind of sense did it make to knock on a closet door? *What is wrong with me?* I thought.

I had turned to leave the room when I heard a thump from the other side of that door. I turned back around and pressed my ear to the door. "Hello?" I whispered. "Is someone in there?"

Nothing but silence.

"Hello?" I whispered again.

This time I heard a soft whimper.

I pressed my ear harder against the door. "Hello? I can hear you. Can you open the door?"

I could tell that someone was trying to answer me, but I couldn't make out the words. Then I heard a sound behind me and quickly turned around. There was no one there, but I knew I'd heard something. I turned back to the door and whispered, "I'll be back." Then I left the room. As soon as I stepped out into the hallway, I ran right into Aunt Terri.

"Oops, I'm sorry," I mumbled as I tried to walk past her.

"Where've you been?" she asked, her tone less than friendly. Her eyes drifted from my face to the open door of the room I'd just left.

"Oh... I was looking for you. I waited in my room for a long time."

"Yes, well, I'm here now. I wanted to talk to you about planning a going away party for you and Abraham. Juan Carlos said you two are planning to leave when Abraham returns?"

I nodded. "Yes. Thank you... for the party."

"Yes, well, I think I have it all planned out so I won't be needing your help after all."

"Oh, okay."

We stood there for a painfully awkward minute before she said, "You can go back up to your room now."

I frowned a little, nodded, and then left.

12

"WAKE ME UP"

That night, I turned all of the lights on in my bedroom and sat at the computer searching the internet for information on Uncle Juan. I found nothing. Was he really that powerful that no one had written an article about him? I mean, he was a drug dealer, and evidently, a big-time one. He lived in a mansion, had bodyguards for every body part. I sighed as I sat back in the chair and rubbed my eyes. I was sleepy but I was determined to stay awake. I wasn't going to let anyone sneak into that room again—not if I could help it.

I sat there and stared at the computer and before I even realized what I was doing, I went to the website I'd been visiting just about every day since we'd been at Uncle Juan's house—the "Find Tomeka Brooks" website. I scrolled down the page and was surprised to see that a new video had been posted. I took a deep breath and then clicked on the "play" icon. Aunt Bobbie Ann's face appeared on the screen. She was sitting on the sofa in her living room and beside her, Uncle Reggie, who was holding my little cousin Faith in his lap. Faith had grown so much, and she was so cute with her chubby cheeks and curly hair. I smiled and touched the computer screen with my finger. My smile faded as Uncle Reggie began to speak.

"My name is Reggie Darrough. I'm Tomeka's uncle. For those of you who have been helping us search for Tomeka, my wife, Bobbie, and I want to thank you and to let you know that we have heard from Tomeka. She called and spoke to Bobbie." He paused and looked at Aunt Bobbie Ann and she quickly shook her head and wiped her face with a tissue. I blinked back my own tears.

I leaned closer to the screen as Uncle Reggie continued. "Um, Bobbie says that Tomeka sounded healthy. We don't think she's been hurt in any way other than the fact that she is still with a convicted felon who is an adult and she is still a minor. Tomeka, if you are watching this, please understand that we love you and all we've ever done is to try to take care of you. What you're doing is wrong. If that man loved you, he would've waited and done things the proper way instead of taking you away from your family. If he loves you, he will bring you home and face the consequences of his actions.

"Thank you for calling and letting us know that you're okay, but you're not really okay, Tomeka. You're not. You belong here with your family. You are still a child. You are not an adult and by now, I'm sure you know you're not ready for the adult life. I pray that you will find your way home. I pray that that man will show you his love by letting you go."

Then the video shifted to pictures of some of my old school friends holding up signs that read, "We Miss You, Tomeka." I was just about to click off of the page when another face appeared on the screen. It was my father's face. From the barred-up window behind him, I could tell he was still in prison.

"Meka, this is Daddy," he said. "If you're watching this, I want you to know that I love you and I miss you and I'm sorry if I ever did anything to hurt you. But now you're hurting your granny. She's always been there for you, Meka, and what you're doing is breaking her heart." He paused and wiped the tears that were flowing from his eyes. "Come home, baby. Ask Abraham to bring you home. He's a good dude. I know he is, and if you ask him, he'll bring you home. I love you."

The screen went black and my heart felt like it had broken into a million pieces. I turned the computer off and stood from the chair. I slowly walked over to the bed and kneeled down beside it, clasped my hands, and closed my eyes.

"Dear God," I whispered. "I'm so sorry for the bad things I've done. I'm sorry for worrying and hurting my family. I'm so sorry. I didn't mean to hurt anyone. I love my family, God. I really do and I miss them. But I love Abraham, too. I just didn't know what else to do because my heart was breaking without him. But now I know that it was wrong to run away, and now I'm so scared. Please watch over me, God, and I promise I'll make things right. I promise I'll go home..."

I finished my prayer and wiped my eyes and then, unable to fight it any longer, I climbed into bed and fell asleep.

***

I wasn't sure what time it was when I heard the noise—a thump or something. I opened my eyes and the first thing I realized was that someone had turned all of the lights off. I felt my stomach bubble and my heart began to race. Someone was in there. I was sure of that. I could feel it, and it scared me to death. I lay there staring into the darkness trying to figure out what to do, but there was only one thing I could do. I had to figure out a way to get out of that room.

Maybe I could ease out of the bed and if I didn't make any noise, maybe I could open the door and run out. It was pitch black in that room. They shouldn't have been able to see me unless they had on some of those night vision goggles or something. I was lying there trying to convince myself that my plan would work when I heard a whisper. I couldn't make out what they said, but I was sure that it was a whisper. All I could think about was Uncle Juan climbing in that bed and touching me. I was so scared, I had to hold my hand over my mouth to keep from screaming.

I slowly sat up in the bed and swung my feet around to the floor. I dug my toes into the soft carpet as I stood to my feet. I moved to take a step when I heard it again—a whisper, but this time, I could tell they were whispering my name. That did it. I wasn't spending another second in that room with whoever that was. I bolted towards the door and quickly snatched it open. Then I sprinted out into the dark hallway. I ran down the stairs and through the wide downstairs hall before stopping to catch my breath.

I looked around to see if anyone was following me, but the hallway was empty and the house was quiet. When I looked to my side, I noticed that I was standing right next to the door—the one with the locked closet. I glanced around me again, checked the doorknob, and then opened the door and rushed inside, locking the door behind me. I decided that that room was a good place to hide for right then. Maybe I could stay in there until the morning. Hopefully, whoever was stalking me wouldn't find me in there.

I walked over to the bed and sat down and thought to myself, *This is the hardest bed in the world.* I mean, it was *really* hard. That mattress felt like it was made out of bricks. I stood from the bed and lifted the covers and then I clamped my hand over my mouth. It *was* made of bricks. Bricks of cocaine or heroin or something. At least that's what it looked like but how could I be sure? I'd only ever seen that stuff in the movies.

I quickly pulled the covers back down and backed away from the bed. I headed toward the door and was about to open it when I heard voices outside the room. I panicked. What if someone, whoever had been in my room, was looking for me? What if they had a key to the door? What would they do if they found me in the room with the cocaine bed?

When I heard the doorknob jiggle, I almost screamed. Then I heard the voices again—two men speaking in Spanish. What was I going to do? Run? Hide? Run or hide where? I couldn't hide under the bed because it wasn't even a real bed. The drugs were stacked from the floor to my waist. My eyes instantly shifted to the closet door—the closet door that was locked earlier. I rushed to it, praying that it was unlocked, and thanked God over and over again in my head when the knob turned and the door opened. I slipped inside the closet and closed the door behind me and almost instantly, a horrible smell hit my nose. I looked around and even in the darkness, realized that I wasn't in a closet. It was another room. I could hear muffled voices, crying, whimpering. I turned around and slid my hand along the wall beside the doorway until I felt a light switch. A part of me didn't want to turn that light on, but another part of me knew I needed to. I turned the light on and slowly turned around.

I gasped and backed up until my back hit the door and then I just stood there with wide eyes. The room was full of girls, all of them naked—some very young, others teenagers, and others looked like grown women. They were all tied up and there were gags in their mouths. Some of the younger ones were crying. A few of them were slumped over, asleep, I guessed. Or maybe worse, maybe they were dead. Then my eyes caught sight of two faces that were very familiar to me. In the corner sat Trinity with tears in her eyes. She was tied up and gagged just like the other girls, but she wasn't naked. In the opposite corner sat my friend from Mexico City, Maribel. I watched as Maribel's eyes stretched wide and she tried to say something to me, but she couldn't because of the gag. I'd started to move closer to her when I felt hands grab me. Before I could scream, someone placed something over my face… and everything went black.

PART THREE: THE SEARCH

(Bobbie)

13

"SEARCHIN' BLUES"

Houston, Texas

A Few Months Earlier…

My days were spent taking care of my daughter and trying to hold my family together. The sadness in Sharee's eyes never seemed to leave. My heart ached and broke for her. She missed her older sister and had even voiced that she felt partly responsible for her running away. No matter how many times I tried to tell her that what Tomeka did was not her fault, she wouldn't believe it. Sometimes I wondered if I would ever be able to make her understand that Tomeka had acted out of selfishness and that the young man whom she professed to love and who professed to love her, was more to blame than anyone. He was an adult and he knew better. I was angry at him—not Tomeka.

Then there was my mother who seemed to grow frailer with each passing day. She practically lived on her knees in prayer. And when she wasn't in prayer, she was cooking or cleaning or taking care of my baby. But since a week or so after Tomeka disappeared, she hadn't even said Tomeka's name. I think that maybe it was too painful for her to talk about her. My mother had been through so much already and she was honestly past the age for raising kids. She was supposed to be enjoying her golden years with my father by her side, but my father was long since gone on and my niece had made her late-in-life parenting duties a waking nightmare.

Thankfully, through the never-ending turmoil that seemed to hang over my family like a dark, ominous storm cloud, my marriage stood strong. Caprice was locked away in a mental ward, hopefully getting some much needed help. They still hadn't caught her baby-stealing aunt, but we had enough security around our house to keep a gnat from intruding, and Faith hadn't been out of my sight for more than an hour in months. And on those rare occasions that I was away from her, she was either with my mother or Reggie. We weren't taking any chances with her safety or with anyone else in our family's safety for that matter.

Besides being worried sick about my niece, I'd had to put my career on hold indefinitely, and that honestly bothered me almost as much as the fact that I had no idea where my niece was or what that man was doing to her. Well, that wasn't entirely true. I had a lot of ideas about what he was doing to her and those ideas woke me up in the middle of the night more than my daughter, Faith's, cries ever had. We'd hired private detective extraordinaire, Martin Miller, to help look for her, but he'd been very blunt about our chances of locating her and what she could be experiencing on the run with an ex-convict.

He'd made it clear that most runaways ended up being plunged into a life of drugs and sex. My worst fear was that she was somewhere addicted to drugs or selling her body to some slimy, disgusting old men. I prayed she hadn't gotten herself pregnant or contracted an STD. But then, there were worse things that could've happened, and I prayed for them not to come to pass more than I prayed for anything else. Martin said she could've been dead by now. I knew that was a very real possibility since we hadn't heard from her in nearly six months. Surely, even in her desire to be with that young man, she would've called to let us know she was alive. Wouldn't she?

To keep from believing the worst, I held to the belief that he was keeping her from calling—that she was being held against her will. That maybe she really wanted to come home and he wouldn't let her. Believing those things was better than believing she was dead or just so selfish that she hadn't bothered to call to ease our worried minds. To believe that she'd be that heartless to anyone, especially her grandmother, was just unfathomable to me.

As the days and weeks and months sped by, we all held each other up. We prayed together and hoped against hope that Tomeka would find her way home soon.

***

"What are you thinking about?" Reggie whispered as he pulled the back of my body closer to his.

I kept my eyes open in the darkness of our bedroom. "More than I want to talk about."

"Tomeka?"

I sighed. "And Mama and Sharee and us."

"Well, we're fine, right? I thought we were good."

I nodded and turned around to face him. "We're good. I just hope it stays that way. Just seems like things will never settle down. What if we never find her? I honestly think it'll kill Mama. I'm afraid she's gonna worry that cancer back into existence. And Sharee... Lord, I just don't know, Reggie. All I know is that I'm tired—tired of worrying and trying to hold things together when they are determined to fall apart."

He rested his hand on my cheek and lightly kissed my lips. "Baby, none of that is within your control. We've got to put this stuff in God's hands, now. We've done what we can. Martin and the FBI are looking for Tomeka. We've got the website up. And your mama is stronger than you think. So is Sharee. And me? Baby, I ain't going nowhere. You can believe that. Things can't get bad enough to ruin us. Remember, I waited a long time to get you back. Dreamed about you for years, loved you through another marriage. I-aint-going-nowhere. And I ain't letting you go nowhere." He pulled me into a deep kiss.

I wrapped my arms around him and returned the kiss, wondering to myself if it was possible for me to love that man any more than I did at that moment.

"We've been praying," he continued once our lips parted. "Now it's time to stand on those prayers and activate our faith. We found Faith when it seemed like we never would, didn't we?"

"Yes, we did," I whispered.

"Things looked bad back then, but God showed up as always. He's gonna show up again. He's gonna move for us. I *know* he is. Something's gonna happen to make Tomeka find her way home. I'm believe that, baby. You've got to believe it, too."

"I'm trying."

He squeezed me tightly. "Dear God, help Bobbie to see your hand at work. Send a miracle our way, Lord. Send our loved one home safe and sound. In Jesus' name, amen."

I tightly shut my eyes. "Amen."

14

"TELL ME MAMA"

We sat across from Martin Miller and listened to his report on the progress that had been made in the search for my niece. This had become a weekly ritual for us. Since Tomeka ran away, Sundays for us had become a day of church, dinner, and meeting with Martin Miller either in person, by telephone, or via Skype. Since he happened to be in town on this day, he met with us in person.

He had no new news to give us, just the same old thing—she and Abraham were most likely in Mexico, but there had been no reported sightings of either of them. The one bit of good news was that there had been no dead black teenage girls found anywhere that fit her description. Though I wished she'd been sighted, I was relieved she was still alive, because the number of bodies that were found every week was saddening and staggering. I could only imagine what those families were going through. I never wanted my family to experience that.

Martin wore a somber expression as he spoke. "I wish there was more I could tell you. I've got a couple of friends—old military buddies—who live in Mexico. They're keeping their eyes and ears open. Tomeka will stand out in some places because there aren't many blacks in some parts of Mexico, but I'm sure Abraham is aware of that. From what I've heard, he spent a lot of time in Mexico as a child and an adult. He was even suspected of smuggling drugs across the border for a big drug cartel at one time, but the authorities couldn't prove it and he refused to testify. He was arrested for possession and received a pretty light sentence. Someone powerful was definitely on his side. I'm thinking that the same person is helping him now. That would explain how he and Tomeka have been able to stay off the radar so well."

I sighed. "I wish someone powerful was on our side."

"Someone powerful *is* on our side, baby," Reggie said softly.

I nodded.

Martin stood from the sofa. "Well, we're gonna keep doing what we've been doing, including checking the activity on the website. If I hear anything, I'll be in touch."

As Reggie stood to escort Martin out of the house, I said, "As always, thank you. We appreciate you, Martin."

He tipped an invisible hat and smiled. "No problem, Ms. Bobbie."

While he and Reggie headed to the front door, I headed out the back door to check on my mother. She usually never missed Martin's updates, but today she'd decided not to be present and had stayed in the cottage on my property that now served as her home. I knocked lightly on the front door before opening it and stepping into the small living room. Sharee was lying on the couch, reading a book.

"Hey, Sharee, is Mama in her room?" I asked.

Sharee looked up from her book and nodded. That's the way she was now—quiet and introverted. She never had much to say anymore and she'd stopped crying the second month of her sister's disappearance. It seemed that she'd gone completely numb to the situation.

"Okay, thanks," I said as I made my way to the back of the cottage and knocked on the closed bedroom door. "Mama? It's Bobbie. Can I come in?"

"Yeah, it's yo' house," Mama said.

I eased the door open. "How many times do I have to tell you that this is *your* home?"

"I know it is, but you and Reggie still da owners. What dat Martin hafta say? Same thang?"

I nodded as I took a seat at the foot of the bed next to her exposed, bony little feet. "No change."

"Humph. Ain't gon' be no change. As long as dat chile don't wanna be found, she ain't gon' be found."

"Then we've got to believe that she will come back on her own," I said, mimicking Reggie's words to me.

"Humph, I spent a lifetime believin' that about her daddy."

I turned to get a better look at Mama, tried to see if her facial expression matched her detached words. She was leaning against the headboard, her tiny frame partially covered with a blanket. Her face was blank. "Mama, I know you haven't given up hope."

She sighed. "Bobbie Ann, listen, I been on dis here earth a long time. Done seen more than you know. I done cried myself out for dat girl. Cried myself out for her daddy before her. I done prayed myself out, too. One thang yo' brother taught me a long time ago, if somebody wanna make a mess uh they life, ain't nothin' you can do ta stop 'em."

I shook my head, still not believing what I was hearing. "This is different, Mama. Junior was an adult when he started using drugs. Tomeka is just a child."

"She ain't no baby, Bobbie Ann. Dat's for sho'.'"

"Mama—"

"I know what you thankin'. Old mean Mama is back. Looka here, I love dat girl like I carried her in my own body. Done raised her from when she was little bitty. Far as I'm concerned, she *is* my child. But I done got old—too old to sit around here holding onto false hope when I done seen the truth over and over again. I done prayed. I believe she safe. But I know she where she wanna be. Dat Mexican boy didn't make her leave. She walked out dat house on her own two feet. She jus' as determined as her daddy. God gon' always protect him 'cause I done prayed for him, too. That's why he still in da land uh da living right today. He gon' protect Meka, too. But I'm telling you, Meka ain't coming back, and if she do, she ain't gon' be no child no mo'.'"

I sat there trying to process what she'd said. I tried to see her side of things. I tried not to feel for Tomeka what I'd felt for myself as a teenager. I tried not to believe that my mother didn't care.

I can admit that there was some truth to what Mama had said. I knew there was. Tomeka had left on her own and met up with Abraham. He had not forced her to leave—not literally. But I was sure he had persuaded her in some way, whether it was with words or manipulation... or sex. Because I knew that sex could be a powerful tool for a man to use—especially against a young girl. Sex to a young girl often equaled love. And I was sure to the depths of my soul that the night Faith was found and Tomeka returned to us for that short stint, she was no longer a virgin. It was written all over her, though she denied it. And when she upped and left, I was even surer. I knew it wasn't his conversation she was running to. It was much more than that.

I stood and left Mama's room, leaving her and Sharee behind without another word. And as I slowly strolled by my swimming pool and into the main house, I wondered if Mama was right. Was I fighting a losing battle in keeping the search for Tomeka alive? I shook my head at my own thoughts. No, this was the right thing to do. She was a child making very bad adult decisions. I couldn't give up on her. She needed to be found and rescued whether she realized it or not.

As I climbed the stairs to my little girl's bedroom, I prayed I would never experience what my mother had experienced and that my heart would never grow cold to my own child.

***

I sat in the living room of my home, laptop in front of me—pen, paper, and recorder in hand. I was doing what I spent most of my days doing—writing song lyrics and softly singing them into the recorder so that I wouldn't forget the melody since I didn't know how to write out the notes. I'd written tons of songs over the past few months—enough to fill three or four albums. I missed the studio and the stage so much. I missed the way it felt to stand before an audience. I missed the feeling of belting out the lyrics to the songs that told the story of my life. I missed hearing the audience cheer and sing along with me, word-for-word. I'd put my career on hold first to take care of my baby girl and now because of Tomeka's disappearance. It just wouldn't have felt right to launch a new album and tour with her still in the wind. But I still missed it—all of it.

I closed my eyes and sighed as I stared out the patio doors at my mother's cottage. I was doing my best to hold things together but I was... tired. *Very* tired. I laid everything down and picked up my laptop. I logged onto the *Find Tomeka* website we'd established just days after she ran away. I checked the site traffic just like Martin taught me to all those months ago. The sight had received over 500,000 page views in total. I navigated to the section that provided a regional breakdown of site visitors. As usual, the southern United States led with the number of views, then other parts of the US, the UK, and Canada. There were also views from Russia and many from Germany. And then I saw something that caught and captured my attention—several page views from Mexico.

I nearly dropped my computer as I grabbed my phone and dialed Martin's number. I virtually screamed the information into the phone. Martin was his cool self, as usual. He led me through a few steps and then had me recite the Mexican visitor's IP address to him. He advised me not to get too excited, that the IP address could trace back to a public computer or some sort of reroute from another computer. Or it could be altogether untraceable for some reason. I took his words in stride, but the hope that had bubbled up inside of me just wouldn't die as I dialed Reggie at work to share the good news with him, too.

15

"CALL ON ME"

My phone never rang in the middle of the night, *ever*. It just didn't. So when it rang that night, it nearly scared me to death. It didn't help that the screen of my phone read *unavailable*. My first instinct was to climb out of bed and walk across the hall to check on my daughter. Caprice's aunt was still roaming around free, and there was always that little fear in the back of my mind that she would somehow break through all of our security and take my little girl again. I answered the phone as I crossed the hall to check on Faith, but the voice on the other end stopped me in my tracks.

"Hello, Aunt Bobbie Ann? It's... it's Tomeka."

Tears sprang into my eyes as Reggie stepped into the hall with concern on his face. "Tomeka?" I croaked. "Where are you?!"

"I... I just wanted you and everybody to know that I'm okay. Don't worry about me, I'm doing fine."

I gripped Reggie's hand to steady myself. I felt so anxious. I felt like I could almost reach through the phone and touch her but at the same time, I felt like she was quickly slipping away. "Tomeka, listen, sweetie. Where are you? I'll come get you no matter how far away you are. Where are you?"

Her voice was shaky as she said, "I gotta go now. Tell everyone

I'm okay. I love you all."

Click.

My knees buckled as Reggie grabbed me and held onto me. "She wants to come home," I whispered. "I can hear it in her voice. She wants to come home."

The FBI had put a tracer on my phone but the call was too short to trace and as Martin said, it was probably made from a burner phone and untraceable anyway. Nevertheless, that phone call renewed my resolve and determination to find Tomeka. Even Mama was a little excited about it. She seemed a little more optimistic about the entire situation, and I was glad she was.

After talking with Martin, I was sure that Tomeka had been at that IP address that he was still researching, and I was sure that's why she'd called—she'd seen the website and something on it, the video or the pictures or the beautiful stories her friends had shared about her, had pricked at her heart.

So I decided we would upload another video to the website's landing page. This time I let Reggie do the talking because I was just too anxious and emotional and excited to do it. We sat side by side, our entire little family on screen, including Faith. Reggie did a wonderful job, as I knew he would. He poured out his heart and mine, too. After we uploaded that video to the website, all we could do was wait and hope that Tomeka viewed it. Prayerfully, it would pierce her heart enough for her to come back home.

***

A couple of weeks after I received the phone call from Tomeka, I woke up early one morning with a very uneasy feeling. Something somewhere was wrong. Everything within me told me that Tomeka was in trouble. I shook Reggie awake and he sat up in the bed, panic on his face. I had no doubt that he was having flashbacks of Faith's abduction as he reached over and turned a lamp on. I watched as his deeply concerned eyes shifted from me to the doorway.

"What's wrong, baby? What happened?" he asked.

"It's Tomeka. I... I think she's in trouble. I just feel it. We need to pray, Reggie. *We really need to pray.*"

Almost instantly he grabbed my hand and squeezed it in his. He prayed for the better part of an hour, pleading the blood of Jesus over my niece, asking God to hide her under His wings and to shield her with His shadow. He prayed for her safe return home. He prayed for our entire family. He even prayed for the FBI and Martin Miller. After we whispered amen, we fell back into bed. It didn't take long for sleep to overtake us. And I slept the rest of the night uninterrupted. For the first time in a long time, I felt like God had heard Reggie and that everything was going to be okay.

***

A week passed with no word from Tomeka or even Martin. For the first time in the more than six months since Tomeka ran away, Martin missed our Sunday update. He didn't call or text or email, and no calls came through on my Skype account. That worried me because I knew it meant that something terrible had happened. I was afraid that something had happened to Tomeka that he was hesitant to share with us. I called him off and on throughout the day to no avail, left several messages, and, when all else failed, I logged onto the Internet to see if something in the world news could give me a clue as to what was going on. Nothing stood out to me.

There was a story about a girl going missing in Mexico City but from what I'd heard, that was an everyday occurrence in Mexico. The drug cartels ran rampant, doing whatever they liked to whomever they liked, so a disappearance was basically par for the course there. But, as I looked at the girl's picture, she reminded me of Tomeka—young and lost. And like Tomeka, she looked as if she'd been forced to learn some things at much too early an age and had had to grow up too fast. Tomeka learned about the effects of drug abuse and experienced abandonment before she even started kindergarten. Then she had to deal with losing my father—the only father she'd ever known. And there was my mother, who ruled with an iron hand and an often unforgiving heart. That was a lot for any adult to have to deal with, let alone a child. No wonder she'd run away. I supposed that, in her mind, being in love with Abraham represented a sense of normalcy.

I logged into the *Find Tomeka* website and checked the page views. There it was again. The same IP address had been back for another visit. I'd reached for my phone to try to call Martin again when it began to buzz. Martin's name flashed across the screen. I was so anxious to talk to him, I nearly dropped my phone in the process of trying to answer it.

Before I could even say "hello" he said, "We found her, Ms. Bobbie. I'm on a plane to Mexico right now. I'm on my way to get her."

PART

FOUR:

RUN

(Tomeka)

16

"LOCKED OUT OF HEAVEN"

I woke up with a dry mouth and the worst headache I'd ever had in my life. I remembered someone putting their hand under the hood that covered my face and then covering my mouth and nose with something that smelled strong and horrible. That was the last thing I remembered until now.

I slowly opened my eyes because it hurt to move any part of my face. When I finally opened them all the way, I could see that I was in the room with the girls. I was sitting on the floor facing them. I looked down at myself and saw that I was naked, too—naked with ropes tied around my wrists and ankles and a cloth tied around my mouth, just like them. I wondered if anyone had done anything to my body. I felt tears roll from my eyes as I wondered what had happened to me while I was unconscious. I closed my eyes and cried into the gag. I felt just as scared as the girls around me looked. I wished I was back home in my aunt's big house with my family. *If only I could just go back home.* If I'd known things would end up like this, I never would've left.

Why had things turned out like this? Was I being punished? Granny used to always quote this Scripture from the Bible when I tried to talk back to her or disobey her when I was a little girl: *"Honor your father and mother—which is the first commandment with a promise—so that it may go well with you and that you may enjoy long life on the earth." (Ephesians 6:2-3.)*

Maybe I'd dishonored my only parent, my granny, by running away to be with Abraham after she told me to stay away from him. I loved him so much, but what good was love doing me right now? He wasn't even with me. And he'd probably never find me in this secret room.

My shoulders hurt from my arms being pulled behind me. I bent forward and tried to pull my hands through the rope but they were tied too tightly. The floor was cold underneath my naked butt and my head still hurt. But more than anything, my heart was beating so fast I was afraid it would beat itself to death, because I was scared out of my mind. What was Uncle Juan going to do to me? What had he done to these other girls? What had he done to Trinity, his own daughter? I opened my eyes and found Trinity in her same spot in the corner of the room. She was staring at me with wide eyes but she wasn't crying like me or most of the other girls. I noticed that her hands weren't tied behind her back. She was handcuffed to some sort of rack or shelf. And her legs were free. It looked like she would've been able to knock that shelf over and escape. I wondered if she'd already tried. I wished we could talk to each other but she was gagged, too.

I searched until I found Maribel, who was asleep. Or at least her eyes were closed. For a second I thought that maybe she was dead, but then I saw that she was breathing. Then I looked at all of the other girls, counted them in my mind. There were 32 girls crammed into that room if you counted me and Abraham's cousin, and my friend. The youngest girl looked like she was seven or eight.

What was this place? Uncle Juan's private stash of girls he molested? Did he take them in that bedroom and dress them up and spray perfume on them?

Those thoughts made my stomach bubble, and I almost threw up into the gag. I thought about all of the days I'd enjoyed eating meals in the dining room or lying in that big bed upstairs with Abraham, being with him. Were these girls down here then, scared and naked and alone? What kind of man would do this? And even to his own child? Did Aunt Terri know about this room?

The door swung open and as two of the huge bodyguards that protected Juan Carlos walked in, my heart started to beat faster, though I didn't think that was possible. They yelled in Spanish as they each grabbed a girl and threw them over their shoulders. Many of the other girls began to whimper as I tried to understand some of what the men were saying. I was only able to understand one sentence, "¡Cállate! ¡Juan Carlos quiere verte!" Or "Shut up! Juan Carlos wants to see you." On the way out, one of them hit the light switch, leaving the rest of us in darkness.

***

I wasn't sure how much time had passed since I'd been stuck in that room crying and listening to the other girls cry, but I was sure it'd been more than a day. I was hungry and thirsty and as hard as I'd tried, I couldn't hold my pee and was now sitting in a cold puddle of it. The longer I sat there the stronger the smell in that room became. Several of the girls had gone number one on that floor and a few had gone number two. I was sure of that because I could smell it. I prayed that my period didn't come before I got out of there. That would be a real mess.

I wondered if I ever *would* get out of there and if I did, what would happen to me? *I should've told Aunt Bobbie where I was when I called her*, I thought. But I had no idea where Juan Carlos's house was located. As a matter of fact, I had no idea where in

Mexico I was at all. All I knew was that they called this place "The Den."

I felt the tears begin to fill my eyes again. I felt like I was having a bad dream but I knew I was awake. I'd never smelled anything like what that room smelled like even in a nightmare. No, this was not a dream. This was real. And I was never going to be saved. I was never getting out of there. I knew I wasn't.

I closed my eyes and began to silently pray, because I knew that only God could help me now. "Dear Lord, I am so sorry for the things I've done. Please forgive me. Thank you for my family. I love them so much. Would you let them know how sorry I am for worrying them? If you can get me out of here, I'll go straight home. I promise. I will go home and I'll never do anything like this again in my life. I'm so sorry, God. I'm so sorry..."

I sat there with my eyes closed and my head hung low and I cried and prayed until I fell asleep.

***

I had no idea what the day or time was when the door slowly opened. The air that came in through the open door filled my nose and I could breathe easier. I heard footsteps and then the door closed again. Whoever it was didn't bother to turn the light on.

"Where are we?" A voice said. I sat up straight. I knew that voice. It was Abraham!

"We're in The Den and Juan Carlos might be the lion, but I'm the lioness, remember?" I recognized that voice, too. It belonged to Aunt Terri.

"Come on, Terri. I'm tired of playing games with you. Why'd you tell me to close my eyes? Where are we? It's dark in here," Abraham said, sounding irritated.

"Somewhere we can be alone and you don't need light to do what you're gonna do," Aunt Terri replied.

I tried to say something but I couldn't. So I moaned loudly, hoping that Abraham would know it was me.

"What was that?" he asked.

"Just one of the girls. Come here," Terri said.

"Is *that* where we are? It smells like hell in here, Terri. Can we go somewhere else?"

"No, I wanna do it in here. Unzip your pants, baby. Auntie Terri missed you."

"I can't get in the mood in here. It smells too bad. Don't y'all bathe these girls? Do people actually buy them with them smelling like this? Damn, it smells bad in here."

My eyes widened. Buy them? And why was Terri calling him baby? What was going on?

"The maids always bathe them before we hand them over to the buyers. They even douse them with perfume and dress them up real nice in the next room. Sometimes the guards even try out the merchandise in that room, if you know what I mean. Now come here. I have missed you so much. I can't wait to have you again. I've been thinking about doing this ever since you came back here," she said.

Then I heard a sound that made me sicker to my stomach than the smell of that room or the thought of Juan Carlos touching me. I heard them kissing. My heart broke when I heard Abraham moan. Then I heard a zipper and I heard clothes fall onto the floor. I wished

I could close my ears or suddenly go deaf so that I couldn't hear the sounds of the man I loved and had run away from home to be with having sex with his uncle's wife. But I was quickly learning that in real life, wishes don't come true. So I just sat there and cried.

They did it for a long time. Longer than I ever remember me and Abraham doing it. Or maybe it just seemed that way because it hurt so bad. And Terri was so loud while she enjoyed my man—*my husband*. All I could do was sit there and cry and moan into that gag.

When they finally finished, Abraham said, "I did what you wanted, now where is Tomeka?"

"It's all about her, isn't it? You love her so much. You used to love me," Terri said.

"Look, we were over a long time ago. Stop stalling and tell me where my wife is so we can get the hell out of here!"

"Your *wife*. Humph, that little girl could never satisfy you like I can, and you know it."

"I love her. She's the *only* one who can satisfy me. Where is she?"

"You're just like Juan Carlos, you pedophile!"

"If you say so. Now tell me where my wife is."

The light popped on, and I looked up at him and her. She was standing there naked, grinning like she was proud of herself. Her eyes were on me. I watched as Abraham searched the room for a few seconds while pulling up his pants. When his eyes finally found me, his shoulders dropped and he shook his head. "You are so evil, Terri," he whispered. Then he rushed to me and began to untie my ankles. I was so relieved and hurt at the same time. I couldn't stop crying.

"What is she doing down here like this?" Abraham asked angrily as he fumbled with the ropes. "She's not one of *them*."

"As long as she's under my roof, she's whatever I say she is and right now she's a nuisance. What did you think would happen if you left her alone here? You know how I feel about you, and you know how I am when something or someone gets in my way. I'm the lioness, remember? Don't you know anything about lionesses? We don't tolerate outside females—*at all*." She reached down and rubbed the top of Abraham's head. "Baby, you don't need her anymore. You belong with me."

Abraham knocked her hand away. "You are crazy as hell if you think I'm leaving my wife for you. Why is she down here? What were you gonna do? Sell her? You must have a death wish."

Terri smiled. "I just wanted to scare her. I don't like her. I don't like that you're with her."

"Yeah, well, I don't like you. I *hate* you."

She chuckled. "Well, what we just did felt like you liked me." She licked her lips. "Felt just like old times."

"Yeah, and I was thinking of *her* the whole time."

Her eyes narrowed as she stared down at us. Abraham finally got my ankles untied. Then he reached behind my head and untied the gag. He kissed me and pulled me to him. "I'm so sorry, angel. I'm so sorry," he whispered into my ear.

I was angry at him and happy to see him at the same time. I leaned against him and cried out loudly.

"Shut her up before Juan Carlos comes down here," Terri said in a harsh whisper.

"Shh, baby," Abraham said. "It's gonna be okay now. Turn around and let me untie your hands so we can get out of here."

I turned around because I definitely wanted to get out of there. "What about Trinity and Maribel and the others?" I asked softly as tears continued to roll down my cheeks.

Abraham freed my hands and stared down at me. "What?"

"Trinity is here, too. So is my friend Maribel," I whispered.

Abraham turned and glanced around the room then he stood and lifted me to my feet. He took his t-shirt off and pulled it over my head. "Terri, what is my cousin doing down here? Does Juan Carlos know his daughter is down here?"

She smiled. "Of course he does. This is her punishment for not following his rules. She's lucky he didn't do worse, and you *know* she is. Cesar's missing and we both know what that means."

Abraham shook his head. "Let her come with us."

She stood there for a moment and then shook her head. "No. She deserves what she's getting. Her little spoiled behind has given me nothing but hell since the day I married Juan Carlos. I tried to be a good stepmother but she wouldn't let me. I'm glad he's angry with her."

Abraham turned his attention to me. "Can you walk?"

I shook my head. "I don't think so. My legs feel kinda numb."

Abraham lifted me into his arms and faced Terri who was blocking the door. "Get out of my way," he said.

She stared at him for a moment before moving to the side. I wrapped my arms around Abraham's neck and closed my eyes, glad to be out of that dungeon.

17

"GRENADE"

Abraham carried me up to our room and sat me on the bed. He grabbed some of my clothes and laid them next to me.

"I-I wanna go home," I said.

"I know you do, baby. I'ma take you home," he said as he began to dress me.

"I stink. I'm not going home smelling like this. I smell like pee. I can smell that room on my skin."

He placed his hand on my thigh. "Angel, we don't have time—"

I slapped his hand away. "I'm not going anywhere smelling like this!" I screamed.

He nodded. "Okay, angel. Okay."

He left and rushed into the bathroom and came back with a wet towel and a bar of soap. I snatched them from him and started washing up.

Abraham walked over to the window. "I know you're mad at me, baby. I'm sorry. I'm sorry I ever brought you here. This was a mistake, a *big* mistake. But I'ma take you home and you're gonna be all right."

"Y-you had sex with her. She-she's your ex-girlfriend, isn't she? She's the one you told me about," I said as I glared at his back.

He nodded. "Yeah."

"She still wants to be with you."

"I know, but I don't wanna be with her."

"Yeah, right."

He sighed. "Angel…"

"I thought Uncle Juan was the one watching us. I bet it was her, though."

He nodded again. "She's just as crazy as my uncle, maybe even crazier, calling herself a lioness, naming this place 'The Den.' I guess that's how they can stay together—being crazy. So, yeah, it was probably her. She's the reason I didn't want to come back here. I *never* wanted to come back here."

"Why didn't you tell me about you and her, Abraham?"

He dropped his head and rested it against the window. "She's my uncle's wife. I was ashamed of myself, angel. I never should've touched her."

I finished washing up and put my clothes on. I could still smell that room on my skin. It felt like I'd never be able to wash it off. That thought made me cry again. Abraham turned and looked at me. He was crying, too.

"She locked me up in that room," I sobbed. "I was down there for days. I thought I was never gonna get out of there. How could you leave me here like that? You *knew* what was going on down there in that room. You knew they were selling girls! You *knew* Terri was crazy and that she still wants you and you *still* left me here! You said you'd take care of me! You said you'd *die* for me! You were lying! I hate you, Abraham!!"

He shook his head. "I love you so much. I'm so sorry, cielito. I'm sorry for letting you down. I wasn't lying, I just made a mistake. Please forgive me, angel. *Please forgive me.*"

I lay back on the bed and curled myself up into a ball. I tightly shut my eyes and tried to cry out all of the hurt inside of me. I felt Abraham crawl into the bed behind me. He pulled me to him and held me tightly and even though I wanted to fight him, I couldn't, because it felt good for him to hold me. We lay in the bed for a long time. I cried for so long that my eyes were sore and my head hurt. I was hungry and sleepy and my heart hurt so badly I just knew I'd die any second. But all I could think about was leaving that place. There was absolutely nothing else in my mind.

I felt Abraham kiss my back over and over again. "Stop," I whispered. I knew what he was trying to do but there was no way I was going to let him do that after what I'd just heard him do with Terri. "Don't touch me, Abraham."

"I love you. I'm sorry," he whispered back.

"I don't care."

Before I could stop him, he rolled me over onto my back and climbed on top of me. He kissed my neck and whispered in my ear, "One last time before I take you home. *Please.*"

"No!" I slapped him as hard as I could. He dropped his head and then looked me in the eye. I slapped him again. And then I punched him in the chest over and over again until he finally grabbed my arms.

"I'm sorry, Meka. *I'm sorry.*"

"You broke my heart," I whimpered.

Tears rolled from my eyes as he held me down and softly kissed my lips.

"Lo siento, angel. I love you so much. Don't you still love me?"

I closed my eyes and shook my head.

"Yes, you do. You're just mad. I only did that with Terri so she could tell me where you were," he said as he started to undress me. "She wouldn't tell me where you were unless I did it. I don't care about her, angel. It's all you. You're it for me. After I take you home, I won't have nobody else. Let me love you one more time. Please. You can beat the hell out of me afterwards if you want. I deserve it. I deserve worse than that."

I opened my eyes and stared at him. For a second, I almost gave in. Then I remembered the sounds Terri made with him in that room. I frowned and spat in his face and slapped him again. "I said, *no!*"

He blinked hard and slid off of me with a sad look on his face. I sat up and pulled my clothes back on. Then I just sat there and shook my head.

"I'm sorry, Meka," he said for the millionth time. He reached for me and I slapped his hand away again. I fought him until I ran out of energy and then I fell against him and cried.

I just cried.

***

"Can you walk now?" Abraham asked.

I nodded as he took my hand, grabbed our bags, and led me out of the bedroom. "What about Trinity and Maribel and those other girls? We need to help them."

"Angel, we gotta get out of here while we can. We can't help them right now."

I stopped. As he turned and looked at me I said, "We *gotta* help them."

He sighed. "How? This place is crawling with people that work for my uncle. We're in danger as it is with what I did with Terri under his roof. We gotta go, baby. We just don't have time for that."

"But we woulda had time to have sex?"

"Angel—"

I let go of his hand and folded my arms over my chest. "Help them, Abraham."

He shook his head and whispered, "Damn-it!" He grabbed my arm. "Fine. Come on." My legs were wobbly as we left the room.

Terri was standing at the bottom of the stairs. As we walked past her, she rested her hand on Abraham's arm. "Your face is all scratched up. Did your little cub hurt you?" She smiled.

I stared at her hand on his arm. Abraham glanced at me and then snatched away from her and kept walking, pulling me behind him.

"I thought you were leaving," she said.

Abraham stopped and looked at her. "We are."

"Then you're going the wrong way."

Abraham turned and tugged on my hand, pulling me further down the hall. "We've got something to do first."

"What?" she asked as she followed closely behind us.

Abraham didn't answer her.

Once we reached the door that led into the bedroom that was connected to where the girls were being kept, Abraham tried the knob. It was locked. He turned to Terri. "Unlock it," he ordered.

"Why?"

He shook his head. "I don't have time for this."

Terri opened her mouth to reply but before she could, Abraham lifted his foot and kicked the door in. Then he grabbed my hand and dragged me through the room.

"Are you crazy?!" Terri screamed as she continued to follow us.

"Probably," Abraham said as we continued through the bedroom.

"What are you doing?" Terri asked.

Still no answer from Abraham.

He kicked the door to the secret room but it didn't give. "Unlock it, Terri," he said.

"Why?" she asked.

Abraham reached into the back of his jeans and pulled out his gun. I gasped.

"I don't have time to play with you. Unlock it," he grunted.

"Or what?" she asked as she put her hands on her hips. "You gonna shoot me?"

"Terri, I've already lost the most important thing in the world to me because of you." He fixed his eyes on me. "I ain't got nothing else to lose, so yeah, I will shoot you if you don't unlock this door."

She glared at me as she reached into her pants pocket, pulled out a wad of keys, and unlocked the door. Once she opened it, Abraham pushed her inside and shut the door behind us. The girls were still there—all of them—and the room still smelled like a dirty toilet. I held my breath as Abraham ordered Terri to sit on the floor.

"One of the guards will be down here any second," she said.

"I hope not for their sakes." He waved the gun in her face and then looked up at me. "You're gonna have to help me, angel."

I nodded.

Abraham turned to the girls and said something in Spanish.

"What'd you say?" I asked.

He turned and pointed the gun at Terri. "I told them we'd untie them but after that, they're on their own."

"But—"

"No buts. I'll do what you want. I'll help them but there's no way they're coming with us. There's too many of them."

"But Abraham—"

"You wanna go home, angel?"

I looked around the room and nodded slowly.

"Then do what I say. Untie one of them and give me the ropes."

I nodded and went straight to Maribel and untied her. "Thank you, friend," she said once she was free.

I tossed the ropes and gag to Abraham and watched as he tied up Terri.

"They need clothes, Abraham," I said softly as I moved on to the next girl and began to untie her.

Maribel moved to the other end of the room and helped me by untying another of the girls. Abraham snatched off the gag he'd just tied over Terri's mouth. "Where are the clothes you keep for them?"

Terri clamped her mouth shut and stared straight ahead. Abraham placed the gun against her forehead. I looked away. "I want you to understand something," he said. "I don't care about you. I stopped caring about you a long time ago. I actually despise you for making me hurt my baby. It would be a pleasure to kill you, so don't play with me. Where. Are. The. Clothes?"

"Wait!" I said. "They're in the next room. I saw them in there."

She said something in Spanish and my eyes widened. I should've figured she'd know the language but I'd never heard her speak it.

"Yeah, well you can go to hell, too," Abraham said to her. Then he turned to me. "I'll be right back, angel."

Maribel and I continued to work to free the other girls. And since everyone we helped, helped someone else, they were all freed in no time. The only snag was Trinity. By the time Abraham made it back with an armful of dresses, I understood why she had not made a run for it. That shelf was much heavier than it looked and would make a very loud noise if we tipped it over. I ungagged her and let Abraham figure out how we were going to free her. He didn't even have to think twice. He walked right over to Terri and snatched the set of keys out of her pocket as she wiggled and yelled into the gag in protest. He quickly found the key and freed Trinity, who walked right over to Terri and kicked her—*hard*.

Then she spat on her. "I've always hated you, you puta!"

Abraham threw some clothes at Trinity. "Get dressed, cousin."

After she'd pulled on a dress, Abraham pulled a gun out of one of his boots and handed it to her. I wondered where the extra gun had come from, but then I decided that if Uncle Juan was a drug dealer with a room full of girls for sale, there were probably lots of guns in that house. "You know how to use one of these?" he asked her.

She nodded. "Cesar taught me."

"Good," Abraham said. "Follow me. Once we get outside the gates, you're all on your own."

"Okay. We can take the cars. There are enough of them to get us all out of here. I'll find out who can drive," said Trinity.

Abraham nodded and turned to me as Trinity organized the women. "We gotta move fast. You still okay to walk?"

My legs were weak and I felt faint because I hadn't eaten in days, but I nodded hesitantly. "I think so."

"Don't lie. I can carry you if I need to, angel."

"No, that'd slow us down."

"What do you weigh? A hundred and twenty pounds? You won't slow me down." He slung both of our bags over one shoulder and then picked me up and slung me over his other shoulder. "You okay, angel?" he asked.

I tried to catch my breath from the quick movement and said, "Yes."

"Okay, baby, when we leave this room, I want you to close your eyes and keep them closed."

"O... okay. Why?"

"Because I don't want you to see me kill anyone. Close your eyes, angel. I love you."

"I love you, too."

With my eyes closed, I heard the voices of Abraham and Trinity and felt Abraham begin to move. He kept one arm tightly wrapped around my thighs. I grasped the back of his shirt with both hands and held my breath—not because of the smell of the room but because of anticipation and fear. I knew they weren't just going to let us leave peacefully, especially now that we'd set the girls free. If Juan Carlos was really selling them, we had just cost him a lot of money. There was no way we could leave without a fight, and with so many of us, we couldn't really sneak out.

I felt Abraham's steps speed up, heard him say, "¡Vamos! ¡Apúrate!"

I was sure he was trying to speed the girls up. But I knew how they must've felt. They'd been sitting on that hard floor for longer than I had, and none of us had eaten in a couple of days that I knew of, maybe even longer for some of them. Their legs were stiff and they were weak. I wanted to explain this to Abraham but since I was the reason they were tagging along and I knew he was already stressed about the situation, I kept quiet.

Abraham suddenly stopped and I heard yelling—many voices, some male and some female. The females were screaming and it sounded like Abraham was arguing with one of the males. More shouting and then... *a gunshot.*

I let out a yelp. "Abraham?! Abraham, are you okay?!"

What was I gonna do if they'd shot him? He let go of my thighs for a second and I thought we were both going to fall. I grabbed the skin of his back. And then I heard a body fall with a loud thud.

"Ouch, baby! What you doing back there?" Abraham asked.

"I… I thought I was falling," I said, my eyes still glued shut.

He gripped my thighs again. "I got you, angel. I got you. Just keep those eyes closed, okay?"

I nodded as my bottom lip began to tremble. "Okay."

He yelled something and then started walking again—then he was running. My head bounced up and down and side to side, making me feel dizzy. I heard screams, yells, more gunshots, bodies falling. It was like I was in the middle of a battlefield in some faraway place. My heart was pounding and my forehead was wet from my own tears. I pulled and twisted Abraham's shirt in my hands and squeezed my eyes tighter shut. When he finally set me down on the ground, I opened my eyes. We were outside, standing next to the car that brought us there. The driver was standing in front of it. Abraham had his gun pointed at him. "Go," Abraham said. "¡Sal de aquí!"

The driver scampered away like a scared puppy.

Abraham opened the passenger door. "Get in, angel."

I climbed inside and took a deep breath. I was a little less scared but I knew we still had to make it out of the gate. I turned and watched as more cars pulled up behind us. *The other girls,* I thought.

"Fasten your seat belt and close your eyes again, cielito."

I did as I was told because I was sure that I didn't want to see what was about to happen. I was glad I hadn't seen all of the chaos I'd heard on the way out of the house to this car. I felt the car jump into action, heard the tires squeal. I gripped my own thighs and mumbled a quick prayer. I'd prayed more in the last couple of days than I had in my entire life. I didn't want to die. I just wanted to leave that place.

Then I remembered something. *One-five-two-three.* "Abraham, I think I remember the code to the gate," I said. "I watched the driver punch it in when he brought us here."

"No, you don't. They change it every day."

My heart fell.

The car jerked to a stop and the silence inside of the car was replaced by the soft sound of a window sliding down. Abraham and another man spoke in Spanish—back and forth. I braced myself for an argument or gunshots, but never heard either. The next thing I heard was Abraham saying, "Gracias." Then the car began to move again. I felt him reach over and gently touch my cheek. "You can open your eyes now, angel."

When I opened my eyes, I could see that Abraham was racing down the highway. The Den was fading in the background.

18

"HOLD ON, WE'RE GOING HOME"

I stared out the window at the desert, ready to go home but not ready to leave Abraham behind. As much as it hurt to know that he'd been with Terri a few hours earlier, I still wanted more than anything to be with him.

We'd been driving for a long time, and I wondered exactly where we were. I wondered exactly where we were going. "Where are we?" I asked.

"A few hours from the Texas border. I'll get you home soon."

"But where are we in Mexico?"

"Um, somewhere in Chihuahua. You don't need to know any more than that."

I nodded as I turned and watched the scenery outside the window begin to change. There were mountains in the distance.

"Do you hate me, Meka?" Abraham asked. "Are you still mad at me?"

I dropped my eyes and stared at the inside of the car door. "I'm still hurt, if that's what you mean."

"I'm sorry."

"I know. You already said that."

"I mean it."

"Yeah, everybody means it. My daddy has been sorry a million times."

"I'm not him, Meka. I'm sorry, angel. I really am. I'm gonna get Terri back for that."

"You're gonna hurt her, for me?"

"I want to."

"How many people did you kill back there?"

"I don't know, baby. I wasn't counting."

"Did you kill your uncle?"

"No."

"*Would* you kill him?"

"If I had to."

"Do you think he knew I was down there with the other girls?"

He loosened and tightened his grip on the steering wheel. "There's not much that goes on in that house that he doesn't know about."

"Except you and Terri."

"There is no me and Terri," he muttered.

"Yeah, whatever."

"Meka—"

"I don't wanna talk about it."

Abraham sighed.

Neither of us said a word for several minutes.

"You knew those girls were down there the whole time, didn't you?" I finally said. "That's why you told me not to snoop around. You knew about that room."

"Actually, I was more concerned about you finding drugs."

"I found them, too."

He dropped his head a little but kept his eyes on the road. "I'm sorry. I shouldn't have taken you there. I *never* should've taken you there."

"Abraham, you didn't answer my question. Did you know about the girls?"

He was quiet for a while before finally saying, "I didn't think it was our business."

I turned and looked at him. "Some of them were just little girls. You think it's okay to sell little girls?"

He shook his head. "I didn't say that. I just didn't think it was my duty to save them."

I frowned. "Whose duty did you think it was, then?"

He shrugged and glanced over at me. "I don't know."

"That could've been me. It *was* me. If you hadn't come back, Terri or your uncle might've sold me to someone. I watched this documentary once about how people buy young girls and make slaves out of them. They make them do whatever they want. They do horrible things to them."

Abraham stared out the windshield in silence.

"Your own cousin was in that room."

He glanced at me again. "I didn't know she was there, though."

"But you knew there were girls in there. You *knew* that. I just don't understand how you could know that and not want to help them."

"Like I said, it wasn't my business."

I turned my entire body towards him and stared at him. "What *was* your business, then? To do whatever your uncle told you to do? To go along with whatever he said? To have sex with your uncle's wife?"

He shook his head. "No! *You. You* are my business—taking care of you. Watching out for you. Loving you. I don't have any room for anything else. I don't care about anything else."

"You don't care about those girls? Not at all?"

"No, I don't."

I turned back to the window, speechless.

He sighed. "I'm sorry. I never said I was perfect, but I love you. I'm not a good person, angel. I never said I was. The only good part of me is the part that loves you. I helped those girls because you wanted me to. If you asked me to jump off of one of those mountains, I would do that, too. I'll do anything for you. You got my whole heart, Meka. There's no room for anything else. I don't care about anything or anyone else. It's killing me to have to take you back. It's killing me!" His voice cracked.

I didn't look at him. I couldn't. I wiped tears from my own cheek. "I don't wanna leave you, Abraham. I'm just tired of being scared. I can't take it anymore. I just wanna feel safe again. I want a normal life again."

"I know. I should've just taken my chances at a hospital. I knew I shouldn't have taken you there. I'm so sorry."

We rode in silence for a while before Abraham said, "I need to ditch this car and find another one. I'm sure my uncle has sent someone to find us."

I nodded and then I turned my body toward the window again and watched Mexico pass us by before drifting off to sleep because, as scared as I was, I was even more tired.

***

I wasn't sure how long I slept, but when I woke up, it was dark outside and Abraham was gone. I sat up straight and strained my eyes in the darkness, trying to figure out where we were. There was nothing surrounding us but darkness. No lights, no cars, no houses. Where were we?

The car was sitting on the side of a little road. We weren't on the highway anymore. Were we in America? Had Abraham just left me in the middle of nowhere? What was I supposed to do now? I really wished I'd asked him to teach me how to drive.

I wanted to cry but I couldn't. I'd either run out of tears or I was just too weak to cry. So I sat there with my stomach grumbling and twisting, and I closed my eyes and prayed that if I was in America, someone would find me.

I jumped when the driver's side door opened. I was relieved to see that it was Abraham holding a sack of something that smelled heavenly. "Eat up," he said as he handed me the sack.

I dug inside the bag and pulled out a Styrofoam plate covered in foil. There was no fork, so I scooped up some beans and cheese with my fingers and shoved them into my mouth. "Where'd you get this?"

Abraham pointed straight ahead. "There's a little community about a mile up this road. I walked down there to check it out. A lady was selling plates of food. I got us another car, too."

I nodded and scooped up more beans. I was finished eating in less than a minute but then my stomach started to grumble. I'd eaten way too fast and had to fight to keep the food from coming back up. As Abraham slowly drove down the narrow road, I stared ahead and gripped my stomach. Soon, we were driving into the small community.

"How'd you know about this place?" I asked.

"I didn't. I just noticed the road from the highway. I noticed it was clear and looked like it was being used so I decided to pull over and check it out."

"Why didn't you just drive in the first place instead of walking?"

"I didn't know what was down here. I didn't wanna put you in any danger," he said as he pulled to a stop in front of a shack-like house. He reached over and squeezed my thigh. "I'll be right back."

I watched as he knocked on the door to the house. Almost instantly, it opened and a small man walked outside. There was a woman and several children standing in the doorway. I wondered what day it was and what time of day it was. It had always been hard for me to keep track of time after we made it to Mexico—not because the time zones were different or anything like that but because the days just seemed to run together since I stayed inside most of the time. My time in that room had definitely made things worse. I knew it had to be close to my birthday. Had my birthday already passed?

A few minutes later, Abraham returned to the car and opened the passenger's door for me. "You okay to walk?" he asked.

I nodded and slowly climbed out of the car. He smiled at me as he took my hand and led me to an old car. It reminded me of my granny's car and that made me even more homesick. I climbed inside and tried to fasten the seatbelt but it was broken so I just laid my head against the back of the seat, closed my eyes, and tried not to breathe in the musty smell of the inside of that car.

"It ain't perfect but I think it'll get us where we need to go," Abraham said as he climbed in beside me. Then he let out a yawn.

"Maybe we should find somewhere to sleep. You look tired," I said.

"No, I'm good. I'ma get you home just like I said. I can rest after I know you're safe."

I turned and stared at the other little houses around us. "What day is it?"

"The twelfth."

"It's... it's my birthday," I whispered. "What time is it?"

"Um, about 2:00 AM. Happy birthday, angel. I wish we could celebrate. I wish... I'm sorry."

"Me, too."

***

The ride in our new, old car was a rough one. Abraham said it was because the tires were bad. The radio didn't work and the silence in the car gave me time to think a little too much. My mind went back to the time when I was unconscious in that room with the other girls. I started to wonder again if they did anything to me other than tie me up.

I glanced over at Abraham. "I think maybe they did something to me back at your uncle's house," I said softly.

He frowned. "Who? Something like what?"

"The bodyguards. They... they knocked me out. I don't even remember them tying me up. What if... what if they did something to my body? They could've. I just can't remember what happened."

Abraham stopped the car in the middle of the highway and stared at me for a long time. He reached over and rubbed his hand over my hair and then he grabbed the steering wheel and laid his head on it. "Do you think they did something to you?" he almost whispered.

"That's the problem. *I don't know.* Do you think they did?"

He lifted his head and looked at me. "They didn't touch you."

"How do you know that?" I asked. My eyes were still dry, but my heart felt like it was crying.

"Because if they touched you, I'd have to turn this car around and kill everyone in that house, including my own uncle. They didn't touch you, angel. You hear me? They didn't touch you."

I didn't say another word. I just sat there and decided that I would believe him because it was better to believe him. It was better not to even imagine what they could've done.

"I'm the only man who has ever touched you," he said as the car began to move again. "*I'm the only man.*" He sounded more like he was trying to convince himself than me.

I nodded and closed my eyes and tried to tell myself not to even think about it anymore. I tried to think about my aunt's house and how happy everyone would be to see me. I thought about my granny's fried pork chops and greens. I thought about watching TV with Sharee. I yawned and wondered to myself how much longer it would take to get home.

"Get some sleep, angel. Don't worry about anything. Nobody touched you. Just get some sleep," Abraham said.

And that's what I did. I went back to sleep.

19

"COUNT ON ME"

It felt like I'd been asleep for days, but it was still dark outside. Maybe I'd slept so hard that it just felt like a long time. I hated when that happened. I sat up in my seat and looked over at Abraham who was asleep behind the wheel. I reached over and shook him. "Abraham, where are we?"

He jumped a little, quickly opened his eyes, and looked out his window into the darkness. "At the border."

"How long was I asleep?"

"A whole day. Are you hungry?"

I shook my head. "I'm fine," I lied.

He smiled. "I don't know why you try to lie to me." He reached into the backseat and handed me a bag of potato chips and a bottle of soda.

"When'd you get this?"

"When you were asleep. It's not exactly a meal, but it should take the edge off enough for us to make this walk. I wish I could just drive you back across the border, but that'd be too risky for me."

"It's okay." I smiled at him as I opened the bag. "Thank you."

"You don't ever have to thank me for anything, angel. Look, I'm gonna try to walk you across at one of the narrow, shallow parts of the river. I'm gonna walk you into a town and then I gotta head back over here to Mexico."

I frowned. "You're... you're coming back? But, that's not safe, is it? Won't your uncle be looking for you?"

He reached over and laid his hand on my cheek. "Well, I can't stay in Texas, and besides, I got some unfinished business here."

I shook my head. "Just... don't come back here. I'd rather you hide somewhere in America than get hurt here. I'll be worried about you."

"As long as I know you're safe, I'll be fine. Don't worry about me. I can take care of myself. I love you, Meka. I really do. If you don't believe anything else, I want you to believe that."

"I do believe it," I said softly.

"And I want you to understand that I only did what I did with Terri because—"

I reached over and put my hand on his arm. "I know. I believe you."

"I'm gonna find a way to get in touch with you. I promise you that."

"Okay."

He leaned over, held my face in his hands, and kissed me for a long time. And after not being able to cry for hours, I felt my eyes fill with tears as I wrapped my arms around his neck and kissed him back. I *didn't* want to go but I *did* want to go. I was so confused, and

I loved him so much.

Abraham ended the kiss and wiped my wet cheeks with his hands. "I love you so much, cielito. I love you *so much*."

I wiped the tears from his face. "I love you, too, Abraham. I don't wanna leave you."

He hugged me. "I know but you gotta go. I'll contact you. I'll find a way."

He let me go and then climbed out of the car. He walked around, grabbed my bag of clothes from the back seat and opened the door for me then reached for my hand. "Come on, angel."

We walked from a dirt road into the brush at the foot of the mountains that surrounded the Rio Grande.

"How do you know exactly where to cross? How do you know we won't get caught?" I asked.

"This is where I used to cross when I was carrying drugs for my uncle. I did it dozens of times. I know this place like the back of my hand. And we just have to be careful so we don't get caught."

I nodded as we carefully, slowly, made our way to the river. The only light out was the moon and that wasn't much light at all. The night air was chilly and the only sound was our footsteps until we reached the river. I could hear splashing as other people, several other people, crossed over from Mexico to the United States on horseback and on foot.

Once we reached the river's edge, Abraham laid the bag on the ground and put both of his hands on my shoulders. "I need you to take your shoes off, baby. Carry them in your hands. If you keep them on, you'll probably get stuck in the mud."

I nodded. "Okay."

"Stay close to me, angel. Stay close. We're gonna move slow and steady. Once we get across, we've got to walk a little ways before we meet the people who are gonna take you to El Paso. Once you get there, you can call your folks."

I shook my head. "No, you said you were gonna walk me into a town. I don't wanna go with some stranger! I want *you* to take me!"

"Meka, I told you I can't go back yet. *Not yet.* I got business to take care of here first. You'll be okay. No one is gonna hurt you again. No one is *ever* gonna hurt you again. I put my life on that." He kissed me again and then he pulled me to him and hugged me so tightly, it felt like he was squeezing the life out of me. But I didn't pull away. I *couldn't* pull away from him. I loved him with everything inside of me. I loved him more than anything in the world and right at that second, I knew I couldn't leave him.

"I'm not going home. I don't wanna leave you. I forgive you for what you did with Terri. Please let me stay with you. *Please*," I whispered.

Abraham backed away a little and squeezed my shoulders. "You've *got* to. We'll be together again. I promise you that. If it takes the rest of my life, I'm gonna make sure we're together again. No matter where you are, I'll find you. I promise I will."

My eyes filled with tears so quickly that I couldn't stop them from flowing. "I'm not going!"

"You've got to!" he shouted. "You can't stay with me! You've gotta go!"

I jumped. He'd never yelled at me before. I backed away from him, sat down on a big rock, buried my face in my hands, and cried.

"I'm sorry, Meka. I'm sorry for raising my voice," he said as he kneeled in front of me. "But you've got to do this. You've gotta go back. Everything I've done has been for you, including *this*. All I wanna do is take care of you. The only way I can do that now is if I let you go. It's killing me to know that we'll be apart, but this is what's best. Please, baby. Let me get you home. *Please*."

I shook my head.

Abraham lifted his shirt and turned his back to me. "Touch it," he said.

I reached up and placed my hand on the huge, black letters of my name.

"See, we'll always be together." He turned around and grasped my wrist. Then he brought it up to his lips and kissed my tattoo. "Always—*siempre*."

I cried harder. It just hurt *so bad*. After all we'd been through to be together, it hurt to know that we'd be apart.

Sitting there next to that river, listening to the water flow, feeling the cold night air, seeing the moon, everything was so real. I was leaving Mexico. I was going back home to my family. I was leaving Abraham behind. And no matter how many promises he made, I knew deep in my heart that once we separated, we'd never be together again. *I knew it.* But I also knew that he was right. I couldn't stay in Mexico any longer. I didn't even *want* to be there anymore. What I did want was Abraham. That's all I wanted.

I looked up at him, wiped my face, and said, "I... I'll go. I know I have to. I know it's what's best."

He grabbed my wet hands and kissed them. "I love you. Don't you ever forget that. *I love you*."

"I love you, too. I love you so much."

Abraham grabbed my feet and untied my shoes. He handed them to me and helped me stand up. "Slow and steady, angel. Okay?"

I nodded.

Abraham carried my bag over his head while he led me across the Rio Grande. The water was freezing cold and reached all the way to my thighs. My legs felt extra heavy and with each step I took, my feet seemed to sink deeper and deeper into the muddy river bed. My whole body was shivering by the time we made it to the other side. It took less than ten minutes to cross the border. Just like that, we were back in Texas, back in the United States.

I put my shoes back on and followed Abraham through the tall weeds and bushes. My wet jeans made my legs feel thick and my stomach was twisting from hunger and fear. It was so cold that I could see my breath in the moonlight.

I didn't want to leave Abraham but I would be glad to get home and out of my wet pants. I couldn't wait to crawl into a bed and go to sleep without worrying about someone watching me. I couldn't wait for all of this to be over. But as ready as I was to go home, it didn't take long for my lack of a real meal to catch up with me.

I stopped and bent over. "Wait. I don't feel good. My stomach hurts."

"I know but we gotta keep moving," he whispered. "We don't need for border patrol to catch us. They'll detain me and I need to go back."

I lifted my head and took a deep breath. "Okay. I'm sorry."

He pulled me by the arm, and we walked for what felt like at least an hour. My legs were tired and the chips and soda had completely left my stomach. I was cold and my head hurt and I had to fight not to cry. And then Abraham stopped. He stopped and stood completely still.

"What?" I whispered.

He shook his head and held a finger up to his lips. "Someone is following us."

20

"TALKING TO THE MOON"

"How can you tell? I didn't hear anything. Where are we anyway?" I was so tired I was beginning to feel frustrated.

"I heard footsteps," he whispered as he pulled me into some bushes.

"Maybe it was someone else who just crossed the border, too."

"Maybe," he said as he crouched down and pulled me down with him. He pulled his gun out of his pants and stared into the darkness above us. I strained my ears, trying to hear footsteps or something. I didn't hear a thing.

"Abraham, you're being paranoid. I don't hear—"

"Shh!" he whispered. "Just be quiet for a minute."

I rolled my eyes. This was stupid. It was dark and I doubted if he even knew exactly where we were. Maybe he was lost and this was his way of playing it off. "Are we lost?" I asked without even trying to whisper.

Before he could answer, I heard a bullet fly over my head and I almost peed on myself. I grabbed him but he shook me off and stood to his feet. "Get lower, Meka!" he ordered. I was done arguing. I did just what he said.

I laid flat on the ground, my cheek against the dirt of the dry desert-like land. Abraham fired his gun and yelled a jumble of Spanish and English. From what he said, he believed these were his uncle's people shooting at us. But how did they find us? He'd been so careful and he'd been sure we weren't being followed.

He ducked back down beside me. "Damn! They must've been waiting for us. They knew I'd try to bring you back over the border."

I raised my head and looked up at him. "How? How would they know that?"

"I don't know. I told Trinity what my plan was. They might've made her talk."

"But she left when we left."

"Yeah, but they might've caught up with her. She's spent her whole life being pampered. She wouldn't know how to survive on the run. I should've brought her with us. She could've stayed with my mother."

"What are we gonna do now?" I whispered.

"When I say run, we're gonna run for it. I'll stay in back since I have the gun. Get ready."

"O… okay."

He reached down and pulled me to my knees. "I love you. If something happens and we get separated, keep running."

"But… I don't know where I'm going."

"Keep running north."

"Abraham, I don't know which way north is. You can't leave me. Please, don't make me do this alone! *Please!*"

"Baby, I don't know what's gonna happen. All I know is that people, *bad people*, are following us and shooting at us and if I get hurt, you've gotta keep going. Promise me that."

My eyes welled up. "But I don't know how to get to wherever I'm supposed to be going, Abraham. *I don't know.*"

Abraham looked up for a moment. "There's a crescent moon. Look up, angel. Let me show you something."

I looked up at the sky, tears rolling down my cheeks. "I see it."

"Stay in the direction of the top of the moon. That's north. Eventually, you'll run into a narrow path. Someone will be waiting for you."

"How will I know them?"

"They'll know you." He kissed me and then pulled me to him. "Ready?" he asked.

"No."

"Angel, we gotta do this."

I sighed and wiped my face. "Okay."

"Go!" he said.

I took off running towards the moon. I could hear Abraham right behind me and I could hear shouting. No gunshots. I ran until the air I breathed in felt like fire. I ran until my stomach began to twist into knots and my feet began to throb. "Abraham!" I called. "I need to rest a second. *Please.*"

He grabbed my arm and almost threw me behind a tree. I fell onto the ground. I sat there and tried to catch my breath but I was too scared to breathe. Too scared to think. I was trembling but was it from the cold, night air that seemed to instantly freeze my wet clothes and skin, or was it from the fear, the terror?

"We gotta keep moving, angel," he said. "Come on, we gotta keep moving. I promise we'll take a break as soon as it's safe."

He reached for my hand and helped me up from the ground. We ran and ran and ran. The sound of the barking dogs made my heart race faster than it already was. *Where did they come from?* I wondered. I hadn't heard them before. And then there were more gun shots. One after the other. I couldn't tell if the shots were coming from Abraham or the other people. I screamed as I covered my ears and continued to run. It was too much. It was all too much. Tears wet my face, almost burning my skin in the freezing cold. I ran until I ran out of both breath and strength. Then I dove into some bushes.

"I'm sorry," I whispered. "I can't run anymore."

No answer.

It was then that I realized I was alone. Where was he?

Seconds later, I heard a scream. A horrible scream. It was him.

They'd caught him.

I listened to him scream over and over again. "Run, angel! Ahhhhh! Run, baby!"

I closed my eyes and hugged my knees and cried. What was I going to do? I couldn't just leave him. I needed to help him, didn't I? I leaned forward and buried my face in my knees and tried to breathe. My stomach jumped and twisted. It felt like I was going to vomit. "Abraham... Abraham... Abraham," I whispered. "No, no, no."

"Angel, I love you. I love you so much. Run, baby! *Run!*"

"I love you, too," I said softly enough for only me to hear.

I looked up and tried to remember what he said about the moon. I asked God to give me the strength and the courage to go on without Abraham. When I finished my prayer I realized the screaming had stopped. As a matter of fact, I heard nothing but my own breathing. I sat there for a long time and still heard nothing. Had something happened to Abraham? Was he... dead? Did they kill him?

My heart jumped and my hands shook as I forced myself up onto my knees. I peeked between the bushes but couldn't see anyone or anything. I closed my eyes and tried to hear something, *anything*. I heard nothing. A horrible feeling hit me all at once—Abraham was gone. One way or another, *he was gone*.

With tears rolling down my cheeks, I crawled out of my hiding place and slowly stood up. I looked around at what I could see in the moonlight, which was not much at all. And then I heard something—a twig snapped or some grass crunched or something. Or maybe it was nothing but my imagination. Whatever it was, it scared me and the only thought in my head was to run. So I ran faster than I ever had in my whole life. I wasn't even sure if I was running in the right direction. For all I knew, I was running straight into danger. But I still ran. I ran until my breathing was so loud I was sure anyone in the world could hear it. I ran until my legs started to cramp like someone was squeezing the life out of them. I ran until my head hurt. I ran until I ran right into a big, tall man who grabbed me and held on tight. I couldn't fight him. I didn't even try.

21

"THE OTHER SIDE"

I was crying so hard; I couldn't even see the man's face or hear what he was saying to me. Finally, he shook me. "Are you Tomeka?!" he shouted.

I blinked a couple of times. He was speaking English. I'd never heard any of Juan Carlos's guys speak English. "Who... who are you?" I asked.

He smiled. "It's you, isn't it? I'm a friend of Abraham's." He turned on a flashlight and shone it on his own face. He was white with dark eyes and hair. With a squint he said, "Where's Abraham?"

I shook my head. "I don't know. Some people grabbed him back there." I pointed behind me. "I don't know if he's dead or alive." I looked up at the man. "You've got to help him. You've gotta go back there and help him!"

He stood there and looked like he was actually considering it. Then he said, "No, I promised him I'd get you out of here no matter what."

"But he might be in danger!"

He shook his head. "No, Abraham is right where he wants to be. Come on, let me get you out of here."

I turned and looked back at where I'd come from. I already missed Abraham, but I knew that the man was right. I turned back to him and nodded. I followed him only a few steps before we stepped onto a narrow road, and a few feet down that road was his car. It felt strange climbing into that car with him. It felt weird riding down the highway listening to an American radio. As a matter of fact, although I knew I was back in Texas and close to home, it didn't feel like home at all. Because in my heart, home was wherever Abraham was. I looked down at my hands and rubbed my finger across my wedding ring. As the sun began to rise in the sky, I wondered if I'd ever get over the pain I felt. Would I ever get over Abraham?

"My name is Danny," the guy said.

I glanced at him. "Thank you for helping me, Danny," I said softly.

"No problem, Tomeka. Anything for my buddy, Abraham." He handed me a wad of money. "I'm gonna get you a room at a hotel here in El Paso. You can use that money to buy some food. Once you get in your room, call home."

I squeezed my hand around the money and looked over at him. "Can we just stop for food on the way there?" I asked.

"Hungry, huh? Sure, what do you want?"

My first thought was to say that I wanted Abraham. Instead, I said, "Taco Bell."

He smiled. "Gotcha."

A few minutes later, I was stepping inside of a clean room at the Comfort Inn, with a sack full of soft tacos and a huge Baja Blast Mountain Dew in my hands. After Abraham's friend left, I sat down on the side of the bed and instead of calling home, I cried.

***

Hours later, I was still sitting on the side of the big bed in my room. I sat there and stared at the phone as if it was the first time I'd seen one. I needed to call home. I needed to call my aunt so that she or my uncle could come and get me. But I just couldn't do it. I think maybe I was afraid to or maybe I was just embarrassed. I had failed. Me and Abraham had failed and I felt stupid.

Plus, I was unsure of how things would go with them. I knew they'd been looking for me, and they said they wanted me to come home. But things were so different now. *I* was different. How would things be with my family now? How would things be with my granny?

I picked up the phone, dialed Aunt Bobbie Ann's cell phone, and hung it back up before it had a chance to ring. Then I closed my eyes and tried not to cry. Why did things have to be so hard? Why couldn't Abraham and I have just lived happily ever after? Why couldn't my life have been normal from the beginning instead of the hot mess it'd always been? And why did I have to meet Abraham and fall in love with him if we couldn't be together? It just wasn't fair! Nothing in my life had ever been fair!

I covered my face with my hands and took a deep breath. Then I picked up the phone and dialed my aunt's number again. This time, I let it ring.

"Hello?" she answered.

My eyes filled with tears as my head filled with more confusion and my heart filled with more pain. "Aunt Bobbie Ann? It... it's Tomeka. I'm in El Paso. Can you come get me?"

***

The ride back to Aunt Bobbie Ann's house was mostly quiet. I sat in the backseat with Sharee who seemed really glad to see me. She hugged me inside my motel room and said she'd missed me. I told her I missed her, too. And I did. I really did. She'd grown up since I'd been gone. She looked more like a teenager than the little girl I remembered. She'd had a birthday, too.

"Sorry I missed your birthday," I said softly.

She shrugged. "It's okay. You missed yours, too."

I guess she was right. My birthday really hadn't been much of a birthday at all.

"I'm so glad you're okay. We were so worried when Martin told us what he and the federal agents found at Abraham's uncle's house," Aunt Bobbie said.

I looked up at her and frowned. "What? What was Martin doing there? What did they find?"

Aunt Bobbie twisted around in her seat as far as the seatbelt would let her and looked at me while Uncle Reggie continued to drive. "Martin's been looking for you—along with the police. He found you through the computer you used to visit our website. He and the police went to that house to get you but you were gone and almost everyone there was... dead. Someone shot and killed nearly everyone in that house, including Abraham's uncle. The only person left was his daughter—I guess that makes her Abraham's cousin. I think they said she has a brother here in the states. He's supposed to be on his way there to be with her. Anyway, I was so scared that something had happened to you, and then you called. Thank God you're okay!"

I sat there with my mouth open. Everyone was dead? Everyone except Trinity? Had Trinity gone back or had they caught her and taken her back? "Was... was Abraham there? Is he..."

Aunt Bobbie Ann shook her head. "No, they didn't find him there. You don't know where he is?"

I turned my head and looked out the window while I rubbed my finger across my ring. "No."

"Well, the FBI think a rival drug cartel killed everyone. But they are looking to question Abraham, and they may want to talk to you, too, since you were there recently. I also need to get you to a doctor to get checked out. To make sure you're okay. But all of that can wait. Unless you feel like you need to see a doctor right now. Do you?"

"Huh?" I asked. I had barely heard a word she'd said. "Um, no. I don't need to go to the doctor. I'm... I'm fine."

"Good. Well, I'm just glad you weren't there at his uncle's house when all of those people were killed. Thank God for that!"

I nodded. I felt strange because I knew in my heart that a rival drug cartel didn't kill those people. Abraham did it. I had no idea how many people he shot when we were leaving, but I didn't think he'd killed everyone and I knew for sure he hadn't killed his uncle then. Now he'd killed his uncle and all of the rest of the people in that house. That was the business he had to take care of. They'd caught him because he *wanted* to be caught. That had been his plan all along—to be caught so that he could go back and kill everyone.

Abraham was a murderer, a cold blooded murderer. I should've been upset about that, but I really wasn't. I was more upset about the fact that now I was sure I'd never see him again. He was probably on the run. He couldn't risk coming back for me. I knew he couldn't. I wanted to cry but I didn't. I wanted to cry alone, not in the backseat in front of my family.

"Are you okay?" Sharee asked.

I looked over at her but I didn't answer. Because I wasn't okay and I wasn't sure if I'd ever be okay again.

"I know this is hard for you, Meka, but I'm glad you decided to come back home. You'll get over him. It'll take time, but you will. I promise," Aunt Bobbie said.

I didn't answer her either, but in my heart I knew she was wrong. I didn't see how I would ever get over Abraham. I just didn't see how that was possible at all.

PART

FIVE:

HOME

(Tomeka)

22

"IT WILL RAIN"

The first thing I noticed when I walked into Aunt Bobbie Ann's house was the smell of my granny's cooking. I would know the smell of her neck bones, collard greens, and cornbread anywhere. Those smells reminded me of growing up in the country. They reminded me of better times and worse times. But most of all, they reminded me that my granny did, at one time, care about me. Was this a welcome home dinner? Would she be glad to see me? Or would she be disappointed and angry?

Uncle Reggie wrapped his arm around my shoulder as we walked into the living room to find Granny on the sofa and little Faith on the floor playing with a colorful pile of Legos. When Granny looked up and saw us, she just sat there and stared. I'm not sure how I felt at that moment. But I guess I felt a little disappointed. Everyone else had seemed so glad to see me when they'd arrived at the motel in El Paso. They'd hugged me and kissed my cheeks. Aunt Bobbie Ann had even cried. But Granny, she just sat there and stared at me like she was trying to figure out whether or not I was real. And I just stood there and stared back because I didn't know what else to do.

I didn't know exactly what to say either, so I just said, "Hey, Granny." And then I bent over and picked Faith up. She'd gotten so big!

Granny nodded a little and said, "Hey, Meka. You hungry?"

I nodded. "Yes, ma'am."

She grunted as she lifted herself up from the sofa. I noticed that she looked smaller. I wondered if she was sick again. "Well, everybody wash your hands so we can eat," she said.

Dinner was quiet. I guess none of us really knew what to say and, although the food was good just like I knew it'd be, I felt uncomfortable. I felt like a stranger who didn't belong there, like I'd left my real home behind when I crossed the border.

As I sat there and looked at the family members surrounding me at the table, I realized that I didn't know them anymore and they didn't know me. Not really. And they didn't understand me. All they knew was that I'd left in the middle of the night and had stayed gone for several months. They didn't understand why I'd left, and I was sure they didn't really believe that Abraham and I loved each other.

I suddenly lost my appetite and pushed my plate away. I slowly looked up at Granny. "I don't feel so well, Granny. Is it okay if I go lie down?"

Granny just looked at me like she didn't understand what I was saying. I got scared for a second. I hoped she wasn't losing her mind like a lot of old folks do.

Finally, Aunt Bobbie said, "You wanna lie down in the guest room upstairs?"

I nodded, picked up my plate, and took it to the kitchen before going up the stairs and climbing into bed. A few seconds later, there was a knock at the door. When I opened it, Sharee was standing on the other side with a laptop under her arm.

"Can I come in?" she asked.

I nodded and walked back over to the bed.

She sat down next to me and set the laptop in her lap. "You okay?"

I shrugged. "I'm all right."

"You're different."

I frowned slightly. "Different like how?"

It was Sharee's turn to shrug. "I don't know. You seem nicer."

I raised my eyebrows. "Oh."

"Nice tattoo."

I looked down at my wrist. "Thanks."

"That 'A' is for Abraham?"

I nodded.

"You miss him?"

"Yeah, a lot," I said softly.

"I like your hair, too."

I shrugged as I ran my fingers through my thick, kinky hair. "Thanks. Couldn't straighten it while I was gone."

"It's nice. Hey, can I ask you something?"

"Yeah, what?"

"Did you have sex with him, with Abraham?"

I wasn't expecting that to be the question. I sat there for a second, and then I said, "Yeah." I didn't see the point in lying to her.

"You miss it now?"

"Kinda."

She sighed. "I'm still a virgin. I feel so lame."

I shook my head. "There's nothing lame about being a virgin. I kinda wish I was still one sometimes."

"You don't like sex?" she asked with a wrinkled brow.

"I didn't say I don't like it. It's just that once you do it, you kinda wanna do it all the time, and then when you don't wanna do it, the guy still wants to do it. It's hard to explain. Anyway, you should wait. Once you do it, you can't take it back. You should wait until you get married."

She nodded and stared across the room for a few minutes. Then she said, "You pregnant?"

"Huh?" I asked, shocked again by her question.

"Granny said you was probably knocked up by now. Are you?"

"Uh... no, I don't think so."

"Oh. Hey, I wanted to show you something."

"Okay."

She opened up the computer, which was already logged on to YouTube. My eyes widened as she touched the screen and a video began to play. It was me, standing in that motel room in Guadalajara wearing nothing but a towel. When I turned my back to the camera, you could see the bottom of my butt. I looked just as scared as I felt.

You could see Abraham's legs as he lay on the floor calling for me. You could see that the room had been trashed. You could see the bed where we'd loved each other.

I sat there and held my breath until I watched myself prop the door up in the doorway, blocking the camera. I took the laptop from Sharee and scrolled down—124,000 views. I gasped and then scrolled down lower. There were tons of comments about me being a whore or about black people always breaking things. "They don't even know what happened," I whispered.

"What happened?" Sharee asked.

I looked up at her. "Do Granny or Aunt Bobbie Ann know about this video?"

She shook her head. "I don't think so. I didn't show them."

I stared back at the screen and then handed the computer to her. I closed my eyes and lay back on the bed.

"Are you gonna tell me what happened?" she asked.

"No."

"Fine. I see you ain't changed after all."

I listened to her leave then I pulled the covers over my head and cried myself to sleep.

***

The next morning, Aunt Bobbie Ann came into the room and woke me up. I sat up in the bed, startled. I'd forgotten where I was. For a second I thought I was tied up in that room again. I could almost smell it.

"You okay?" she asked.

"Um... yeah. W... why?" I stammered.

"You looked a little scared."

I rubbed my eyes and yawned. "I'm all right."

"We need to talk, Meka. A lot has happened since you've been gone. Some things have changed."

I frowned as I sat up straight in the bed. "What is it?"

"Uncle Reggie and I are going to be your legal guardians as soon as all of the paperwork is done."

I frowned. "What? Why?"

"We all think things will be better this way."

"Granny thinks so, too?"

She nodded. "She's tired, Meka, and everything that's happened took a lot out of her. We talked and we agree that this is for the best."

"What about Sharee?"

She looked away from me. "Nothing will change for Sharee. Just you."

"So it's only me she doesn't want. She's just tired of me. Not Sharee."

"She's not tired of you. She's just tired, *period*. She's not getting any younger, Meka. And, well, you didn't make things any easier for her."

I looked down at the blanket covering my legs. "So what does this mean? She doesn't want anything to do with me anymore?"

She shook her head. "No, sweetie. It just means that Reggie and I are responsible for you now. I'll have to enroll you in school here and buy your clothes—stuff like that."

I stared at the window across the room. "She's mad at me. I know she is. I could tell when I first walked in the door. She didn't have anything to say to me. She didn't act like she was even glad to see me. It was like... it was like nothing happened."

Aunt Bobbie Ann sighed. "I think that's just her way of coping with things. It hasn't been easy for us, Meka, wondering if you were dead or alive. Praying that you were somewhere safe. And Mama's already been through so much with your father. It was hard for her."

I climbed out of the bed and stood next to it. "It was... it was hard for me, too!"

Aunt Bobbie Ann gave me a shocked look. "Tomeka, you chose to leave, right?" Then her expression changed and her eyes grew wider. "Or did Abraham force you?"

I shook my head. "No, he didn't force me. I chose to go, but it was still hard."

She sighed again. "It was hard because that was a consequence of your own actions. *You* made those choices. And your choices affected a lot of people other than you."

I crossed my arms at my chest. I knew she was right, but I felt like she wasn't trying to see things from my perspective. Maybe life had been hard for them, but it had been hard for me, too. Life had always been hard for me.

"I wanna talk to Granny," I said.

Aunt Bobbie Ann looked at me for a minute as if she was deep in thought. Then she said, "She's in the kitchen, fixing breakfast."

I was still wearing the clothes I came home in when I walked down the stairs and into the kitchen. I could smell bacon cooking and my stomach began to growl. "Good morning, Granny," I said softly.

She didn't respond.

I raised my voice a little. "Good morning, Granny."

She turned and glanced at me. The she turned back to the stove. "Good mornin'. Breakfast is almost done. Be a few mo' minutes."

"You need some help? I can cook a few things now."

"What? Mexican stuff?"

"Some of it is Mexican stuff, but it's good."

"Naw, I don't need no help."

I bit my bottom lip. "Okay. Um, can I talk to you for a minute?"

"About what?"

I sat down at the kitchen table. "About why you don't want me no more," I said, tears filling my eyes.

She flipped the bacon in the skillet, wiped her hands on her apron, and then turned to face me. "Whatchu mean by dat?"

I laid my hands on the table and stared at them. "Aunt Bobbie Ann said you're giving her custody of me. Why?"

She turned the stove off, walked over to the table, and sat across from me. "You sho' you wanna talk to me? 'Cause I ain't got nothin' too nice ta say to ya'."

"Yes, ma'am. I'd like to know why you're throwing me away like my daddy and mama did." I had never talked to Granny like that before, but I was hurt. I never thought she'd just give me away.

She folded her hands together on the table and leaned back in her seat. "I'm letting Bobbie Ann take over raisin' you cause I can't do it no mo'. You thank you grown, now. Maybe you *is* grown now. You been layin' up wit' a grown man for months. You leff' here and didn't even thank to call for a long time. I don't thank you even wanna be here. I don't thank you had no other choice but to come back. And I thank you gon' leave again first chance you git. 'Cause you still cawl yourself in love wit' dat man."

I dropped my eyes. She'd said nothing but the truth.

"Mm-hmm. I know I'm right. If dat boy get in touch wit' you, out da door you goin' again. I know you is, and I'm jus' too old and too tired ta go through dat again. I did my best ta take care of you and Sharee and what you did showed me jus' how much you don't appreciate it. So, I'm through, I'm done. I'ma raise Sharee on up and after that, I'll help Bobbie Ann wit' her family if she want. Shoot, I might even move back home one day. But I'ma tell you what I ain't never gon' do again. I ain't never gon' try to be a mama ta nobody who thank they don't need one."

I felt the tears as they rolled down my face. "I… I never said I didn't need a mother. I never said I didn't appreciate you, Granny."

"You ain't had to say it. You showed me how you felt when you ran off and didn't look back. I can't raise you no mo'. That's all it is to it. Bobbie willin' to try, so she can try. I jus' hope you don't break her heart like you done broke mine." Her voice trembled a little when she said that last sentence, and that's when I realized what was going on. She was hurt. She was so hurt that she didn't want to be my guardian anymore. For the first time, I actually felt like Granny loved me. I'd never felt that before.

"I'm sorry, Granny. I'm sorry for hurting you," I said as I wiped my face.

She stood from the table and walked back over to the stove. "I know you is. I'm sorry, too. I'm sorry thangs is da way they is. I'm real sorry about dat. All I can do is git on my knees and pray for better. You need ta do da same."

I sat there and watched her cook for a few more minutes before I went back up to the guest room, laid across the bed, and cried myself back to sleep.

***

I spent most of that day in bed. I told Aunt Bobbie Ann that I didn't feel well when she called me back down for breakfast. I was sure she knew that I was just still upset about Granny handing me over to her like I was an outfit or a pair of earrings. It hurt, but the more I lay there thinking about it, the more I knew that maybe it would be okay. Aunt Bobbie Ann was kind and so was Uncle Reggie. They'd always been there when me and Sharee needed them and I'd always known they loved me. I couldn't say that for Granny. Well, I guess I knew it, but she just wasn't good at showing it.

That afternoon, I skipped lunch and decided to unpack the bag I'd carried across the border with me. My eyes nearly jumped out of my head when I unpacked the last piece of my clothing and found a note folded up and sitting at the bottom of the bag. I was sure it was from Abraham. I wasn't sure when he'd snuck it into the bag, but I knew it was from him. The door was already closed and I didn't bother to lock it, because I knew no one would bust in on me. I had a feeling that no one wanted to be around me that much or maybe they just didn't know *how* to be around me anymore.

I sat down on the bed and unfolded the note and almost cried when I saw Abraham's handwriting. I hugged the paper to my chest before wiping my wet eyes and reading the note:

Dear Tomeka,

Hopefully, you are already back in Texas as you read this letter. First of all, I want to tell you that I love you. I love you, my angel, and I will always love you. Nothing can change that. The second thing I need to tell you is that I was wrong to take you away from your family. It was wrong and I'm sure that's why we've run into so much trouble. I should've waited for you, but I was afraid you wouldn't wait for me. I was afraid that if we waited until you were eighteen, you'd find someone else, someone your age, and you'd forget about me. I just couldn't deal with that if it happened. So I took you away.

I'm sorry for what you went through at my uncle's house. I'm sorry for what I did with Terri. I'm sorry for the way she treated you. But I want you to know something, I'm going to fix it so that she can never hurt you again. No one will ever hurt you again as long as I'm living. I promise you that.

I love you and for now, I want you to learn how to live without me. I know it'll be hard. It'll be hard for me, too. But this is what we have to do. Don't forget my promise to you. I meant that. No matter what happens, no matter how much time passes, please remember what I promised you.

Love,

Abraham

23

"SHOW ME"

I answered the knock at my bedroom door to find Uncle Reggie standing on the other side with little Faith in his arms.

"You've been holed up in this room for quite a while now," he said. "You wanna come out and join the world?"

I shrugged as I sat on the side of the bed. "It's only been a couple of days and I didn't think the world would want me around."

"Well, we do." He sat down beside me. Faith crawled out of his lap and onto the bed.

I looked over at him. "I guess I'm trying to figure things out."

"Things about Abraham? Your granny?"

I nodded. "Things are so different now. I don't know how to feel."

He placed his hand on my shoulder. "I understand. You wanna talk about anything? I'm willing to listen."

I folded my hands in my lap and shook my head.

"You sure?" he asked.

I nodded.

"Okay. When you're ready to talk, let me know."

He stood from the bed and picked Faith up. As he walked toward the door, I said, "Wait, can I ask you a question?"

He stopped and turned back around. "Sure."

"Do you… do you think God really forgives people for doing bad things, like *really* bad things?"

He nodded. "I know He does if the person repents."

"Do you think He'd forgive me for loving Abraham? Because I still love him. I… I can't stop."

He tilted his head to the side. "Loving him is not a sin. Disobeying your grandmother is a sin. And if he and you did other things together, things that only a husband and a wife should do— that would be a sin, too."

I didn't bother to tell him that we'd gotten married. After all, we definitely did stuff together before we got married. "Well, will He forgive me for… for doing those things?" I asked.

"If you're truly sorry for doing them and you ask Him to forgive you, He will."

"Um, good. What about Abraham? He… he did some bad things to protect me."

"The same rule applies. He's got to repent for his own sins, *all of them*—including taking you away."

I dropped my eyes and focused on my own feet. "Okay."

"You want me to stay? We can talk about whatever you want."

I shook my head. "No, that's all I wanted to know. Thank you, Uncle Reggie."

"You're welcome."

***

A few days after I got back, the FBI came and asked me a bunch of questions about Abraham and the stuff that happened at The Den—did Abraham force me to leave home? Was I, at any time, held against my will? Did Abraham hurt me? Did I know where he was now? Did anyone else hurt me? Did I have any idea who might've wanted to kill Uncle Juan? I told the truth about some things, lied about others. What was the point in me telling them about me being kept in that room? I was free now, and the people who put me there were dead.

Next was a trip to Aunt Bobbie Ann's doctor who said that I was healthy, and no, I wasn't pregnant or "knocked up" as Granny put it. And I guess Aunt Bobbie Ann thought I was a crackhead because they tested me for drugs, too, but they didn't find any. The doctor said I was physically fine—barely a scratch on me, but he couldn't see inside my mind. I dreamed about the room, the girls, and the smells every night. Sometimes I would wake up crying. Other times I would wake up screaming. There were times when Aunt Bobbie Ann would have to rock me back to sleep in her arms. When she asked me what the dreams were about, I told her it was too horrible to talk about. I didn't want to talk about it. I didn't want to think about it, either, but I couldn't stop the dreams.

The first time I woke up screaming, she and Uncle Reggie came running into my room like the house was on fire. I think I really scared them. By the fourth or fifth time, Aunt Bobbie Ann apologized to me. She said, "You said things were hard for you in Mexico. I'm sorry. I should've listened." She asked me again to tell her about the dreams but I just couldn't.

I would see Maribel's face in my dreams and wonder where she was and if she was safe. I would see her little brother's face sometimes even when I was awake, and I would cry for him. And then I started missing Abraham so badly that I could barely breathe. My heart and my mind ached, and the thought of living another day without him was almost too much for me. I probably would've ended my own life if I didn't believe that we'd be together again one day, if he hadn't promised to find me. That was the only thing that made it okay to go on living.

When Aunt Bobbie Ann told me I'd have to see a therapist, I got a little upset. It wasn't like I was crazy or anything. I just had some bad memories that I was sure would eventually go away, and I missed Abraham a lot. But since I refused to talk to her, she said I had to talk to someone. So she signed me up to visit a therapist twice a week.

The therapist was a short, pale-skinned white lady who looked old and out of touch. I wondered how she was going to be able to help a young black girl like me with anything. But she was nice and her smile made me relax a little. Her name was Anne Frank, for real, but she was a Christian counselor. That was so strange to me.

For the first two visits, I basically just listened to her talk and answered her questions with one or two words. The third visit was going the same way. She was doing all of the talking and I was pretty much just staring at the floor.

"Tomeka, I know there is something you need to talk about. I can see it in your eyes. You're safe here, you know? Whatever you tell me won't go any further than this room."

I sighed and moved my eyes from the floor to the wall.

"Things can get better for you if you share them. Keeping them bottled up inside of you will only make them worse."

I kept my eyes on the wall.

"Are you afraid to talk to me? Is that it?"

I sighed again.

"Do you think I won't understand?"

I looked up at her. "I *know* you won't. How could you? Nobody does. Nobody understands me at all."

"Will you give me a chance to try to understand?"

I looked away again.

"How about this? Tell me one thing about you that you think I won't understand. Just one thing."

I leaned back in my chair and crossed my arms over my chest. "Okay. You couldn't understand how it was for me growing up the daughter of two crackheads."

She raised her eyebrows. "No, I never experienced that but you can help me understand. Tell me how it was growing up with them."

I rolled my eyes. "I don't know. They were too messed up to raise me and my little sister so my grandparents did it."

"All right, and how was life with your grandparents?"

"It was okay. I guess it was pretty good until my grandfather died. My grandmother took good care of us, but she ain't never been real nice. But I guess she wasn't mean, either. She was just there and that's more than I can say for my parents…"

I told her a lot about my life that day, about how I felt about different things, and I have to admit that it felt good to get some of that stuff out. It felt good to know that she was actually listening to me even if she might not have truly understood what my life was like.

***

My fourth week back home, my therapist decided to have a session with my entire family except for Uncle Reggie who stayed at home to watch Faith. I just couldn't believe that Granny agreed to come. I wondered how Aunt Bobbie Ann pulled that off. We all sat in a circle in Dr. Frank's office. Dr. Frank even got the prison to let my dad call in. I didn't know what we were going to talk about, but I felt nervous sitting in that room with all eyes on me.

"Okay, well, I'm glad you all could make it," Dr. Frank said.

Aunt Bobbie Ann nodded and smiled a little. Sharee nodded, too, but she didn't smile. Granny didn't move a muscle or say a word. She just sat there with her legs crossed at the ankle and her hands folded in her lap, staring at the floor. For a minute there, I thought she was asleep.

"As Tomeka can tell you, I like to begin each session with prayer."

Everyone nodded this time, including Granny. I guess the word "prayer" had caught her attention.

"Great, let's get started. Mr. Brooks, can you hear us okay?"

"Um, yes, ma'am," my father's voice came from the speaker phone that was sitting right behind Dr. Frank on her desk.

"Dear Lord," Dr. Frank began. "I ask that you fill this room with your presence and that you touch each and every one of these souls in attendance here today whether physically or via telephone. I pray that you open up the lines of communication between these, your precious people. I pray that they all will know healing and restoration today. In Jesus' holy name, Amen."

Everyone said "amen," including my daddy.

Dr. Frank nodded her head and smiled. "All right, let me first tell you all that this is a safe zone. Anything said here stays here. No one is to attack anyone else. We are just going to have some dialog and see if we can all see things more clearly and maybe understand each other's point of view."

Me, Sharee, and Aunt Bobbie Ann nodded and agreed. My father said, "I understand." Granny just grunted and sighed.

"Okay, Mr. Brooks, I'm going to start with you. I know it's been a while since you talked to Tomeka and that you haven't seen her since she's been back home. What is the first thing that pops into your mind to say to her right now?" Dr. Frank asked.

He cleared his throat. "Um, I wanna say that I'm sorry I haven't been the best father. But I've been real worried about you, and I'm glad you're back home and safe and everything."

I stared at the phone.

"Okay, Tomeka, what's the first thing that pops into your mind to say to your father? I want you to be totally honest," Dr. Frank said.

I continued staring at the phone.

"Tomeka?" she said.

"You really want me to be honest?" I asked.

She nodded.

"Well, I don't believe he's really sorry," I said.

She shook her head. "Don't say it to me. Say it to him. Remember, this is a safe zone."

I sighed softly. "Okay… I don't believe you're sorry, Daddy. And I don't believe you were worried." I suddenly wanted to cry.

"Well, I *am* sorry, baby girl. I'm real sorry and I was worried sick. You can ask your auntie. I was calling up there all the time to see if they'd heard anything about where you were. I was going crazy in here," he said.

I held in my tears. "I just don't believe you. I just can't. You were never there for me and Sharee. Even when you tried to be there for us, you messed up. You *always* messed up. I can't believe you. I can't let you let me down again."

"Meka, listen, I know I messed up a lot of times, and I understand why you don't believe me. All I can do is give you my word that I mean what I say. I love you, Meka. I really do." His voice broke. He was crying.

I looked up at the phone again and then over at Sharee. She was crying, too.

The room was quiet for about three minutes. Finally, Dr. Frank said, "Mr. Brooks, is there anything else you want to say to Tomeka before I move on to your sister?"

"Uh…no. That's… that's all. I mean, I love you, Meka. I really do. And I'm real sorry about how things have been for you because of the stuff I did," he replied.

She looked at me. "Tomeka? Do you want to say anything else to your father?"

I believed he was sad at that moment, but my heart and my mind wouldn't let me believe anything else about him. I couldn't believe in him if I'd wanted to. There was nothing else for us to say to each other. So I shook my head and said, "No, ma'am."

She turned to Aunt Bobbie Ann. "Mrs. Darrough, what would you like to say to Tomeka?"

Aunt Bobbie Ann had tears in her eyes when she turned and looked at me. "Meka, I know you think we're all angry at you about running away, but I want you to know that I'm not angry with you at all. I know you thought you had no other choice because you had feelings for Abraham. I just want you to know that what you did affected all of us, not just you. I want you to take responsibility for your actions."

Dr. Frank looked at me and nodded, letting me know that it was my turn to talk.

After a few seconds, I said, "I'm glad you're not mad at me, Aunt Bobbie Ann. But I don't think you really understand how I feel. I really loved him. I still do. Just like you love Uncle Reggie and he loves you. That's how me and Abraham feel about each other. We even got married in Mexico because we love each other so much."

"Married?! I saw that ring on your finger, but married? I just can't believe it," Aunt Bobbie Ann said.

"Lawd Jesus," Granny muttered.

Sharee gasped.

My daddy said, "What?!"

"We got married in a church in Mexico. It wasn't legal, but we did it in front of God so that's all that matters," I said.

"Tomeka, I don't know what to say," Aunt Bobbie Ann said.

I shrugged. "It's what we wanted to do."

Aunt Bobbie Ann leaned forward. "That's just it, Tomeka. All you've thought about in this is yourself and what you wanted to do. What you did tore this whole family apart. Can't you see that?"

I shook my head. "I didn't think anyone would really miss me. I didn't think I mattered all that much to anyone."

Aunt Bobbie Ann sat up straight. "Why in the world did you think that? Of course you matter to us. You matter to all of us!"

I felt more tears fill my eyes. "You're busy with Uncle Reggie and Faith and your music. I was sure you wouldn't miss me."

"Meka, I haven't worked since you left. I put all of that on hold because I wanted to focus all of my energy on finding you."

I looked up at her. "You did?"

She nodded. "Yes. I hired someone to put up that website, I did interviews, I even hired Martin Miller to work around the clock to find you and he did, but you'd already left. Finding you was my top priority."

I felt a tear roll down my cheek. "Thank you for doing all of that, Aunt Bobbie Ann. I'm… I'm sorry. I didn't know."

Aunt Bobbie Ann stood up and walked over to me. She bent over and hugged me. "I love you, Meka. I would've done anything to find you."

We hugged and cried for a few minutes before Aunt Bobbie Ann went back to her seat.

"Are we okay to move on to Sharee or do you all want to take a break?" Dr. Frank asked.

Everyone agreed to move on.

"Okay, Sharee," Dr. Frank said. "What would you like to say to your sister?"

Sharee looked over at me and took a deep breath. "I'm glad you're back, Meka."

I smiled at her. "Thank you."

"Sharee, is that all you'd like to say?" Dr. Frank asked.

"I guess."

"You guess?"

Sharee shook her head. "No, I guess that's not all."

Dr. Frank nodded at Sharee. "Go ahead. You're safe to say whatever you need to say."

Sharee looked over at me again. "I want to say that I hated the way you treated me before you left. I hated the way you acted like I was in the way all the time. You always acted like you were the only one that bad stuff happened to. It happened to me, too, Meka. Daddy is my daddy, too, and Mama was my mama. I lost my granddaddy the same time you lost yours. But you always acted like I didn't have any feelings.

"For a little while, I was kinda glad you were gone because at least you weren't around to treat me so bad. Then, I got jealous. I thought that you were gone somewhere having fun with Abraham and I still had to go to school and stuff. But when you came back, you looked like you had been through some bad stuff and then you started having those bad dreams. I kind of felt sorry for you, then. I kinda knew you had got yourself into trouble."

This time, I didn't even try to hold my tears back. "I… I didn't know I made you feel like that. I'm... I'm sorry. I just wanted to be happy, and I didn't think you wanted to be around me anyway. I guess I was right, but it was my fault that you didn't. I'm sorry, Sharee."

"It's okay. What happened to you? I wish you'd tell me. I remember we used to talk all the time."

I dropped my head. "I saw a lot of bad stuff in Mexico. A lot of stuff I'm trying to forget."

"Stuff Abraham did?" Sharee asked.

"Him and other folks."

Sharee nodded.

"I promise I'll tell you. I will."

"Okay," she said.

Next, it was Granny's turn. "Mrs. Brooks, is there anything you'd like to say to Tomeka?"

Granny kept her eyes on the floor. "I done said everything I need ta say ta her already. She know how I feel."

Dr. Frank looked at Granny for a second and then I guess she figured out that Granny wasn't someone you could persuade to do things, so she turned to me. "Tomeka?"

I sat there for a minute and wondered if there really was such a thing as a safe zone when it came to Granny. I doubted it, but I figured I didn't have anything to lose, she'd already given me away.

"Why'd you give up on me, Granny?" I asked softly.

Granny looked over at me. "We done already talked about dis. No sense in bringing it back up jus' cause we in dis office wit' dis white woman."

Dr. Frank bugged her eyes but she didn't say a word.

I shook my head. "I'm not talking about that. I'm talking about before I left, when we were back home. You stopped caring about what I did, let me miss church and stuff. That's why I didn't think you'd care about me leaving. You'd already given up on me. It was like you had stopped caring about me."

Granny frowned. "Is dat what you thought? Meka, I'ma old woman. I'm tired and maybe I'm a little slack wit' raising y'all now, but I thought you was a good girl. If you didn't wanna go to church sometimes, I jus' let it slide. I knew you was upset about yo' daddy, but I didn't know you was unhappy enough ta run away. I thought you was gon' be okay. And Lawd in heaven know I never woulda dreamed you was talking to a man dat was in prison. I jus' thought you was smarter than dat."

"Why does falling in love make me dumb?" I asked.

"Falling in love ain't dumb, chile, but falling in love wit' an inmate is. You didn't know nothin' about him."

"I knew I loved him and he loved me and that's all that mattered."

She shook her head. "Baby, if love was enough, yo' granddaddy would still be here, cause I sho' nuff loved him. But love ain't enough. It take a lot more than love to make things right."

"I don't understand."

"I know you don't. Dat's what I been tryna git you to see. It's a lot you don't understand 'cause you ain't lived long enough to understand it. You love him. I do believe dat. I even believe dat he might love you, too. But wit' love, you gotta have some sacrifice. He shoulda sacrificed being with you to let you grow up and really know what you wanted in life. You shoulda sacrificed being with him to grow up and live life a little first. Ain't nothin' wrong wit' love, baby. But jus' like everythang else, love got a time. You can't rush it. Da two of you was rushing it, and that's why you back here now."

For the first time, I understood what Granny had been trying to tell me all along and for the first time, I realized just how my actions had affected my family.

"Tomeka, I'll let you have the last word for this session. Is there anything else you want and/or need to say to your family?" Dr. Frank asked.

I sat there for a moment and then I said something that I'd been wanting to say for a long time. "Yes…um, I want to say I'm sorry, again, for running away and worrying everyone. It was wrong and I paid for it and I'll never do anything like that again. I learned my lesson. I… I just didn't think anyone really cared about me. I really didn't. But now I see I was wrong. Me and Abraham shoulda waited. I know that now. But I… I was afraid I was gonna lose him forever and I guess now I really have lost him forever. I know we'll never be together again and that really hurts.

"I just wish you all understood that what me and Abraham had was real—that we really loved each other. I *still* love him. I always will. And I miss him every day. It's hard… it's so hard to love someone that you can't be with. It hurts when I know that loving him is wrong but at the same time, I can't help it. I can't stop loving him.

"You keep saying stuff like 'you'll get over him' or 'you don't know what love is.' But how do you know what I feel inside? How could you know that? I love him and he loves me. He wasn't perfect, but he took care of me and that's more than I can say for my own parents. Sorry, Daddy, but it's the truth." I didn't wait for my father to reply. I just kept talking. "He protected me, and I know there's nothing he wouldn't do for me. I know that's love. Why can't any of you see that?"

There was a minute of silence until Aunt Bobbie Ann said, "I see it, Tomeka. I really do."

"Thank you, Aunt Bobbie Ann."

No one else spoke.

I wiped my wet face and sighed. "Okay, I wanna tell y'all about Mexico now if that's okay."

Everyone nodded and stared at me as I told them about my life in Mexico—the good and some of the bad. I even told them about the video of me wearing nothing but a towel in that motel room. Nobody said "I told you so." Not even Granny. They just listened. And when we left Dr. Frank's office that day, I felt so much better.

EPILOGUE

I walked through my old house in Willisville and smiled. For the longest time when I was a girl, I'd wished to get away from that place, but at that moment, I couldn't think of a better place to live. Like most people, I couldn't appreciate my home until I'd been away from it and came close to never seeing it again. Of course, things were different than before. Granny and Sharee were still in Texas. I was alone, but I wasn't afraid. This place felt more like home than anywhere else in the whole world. I'd actually missed the quietness. I'd missed hearing the choir practice on Saturday mornings. I'd missed going to church and sitting on Granny's favorite pew.

I was eighteen, I was a high school graduate, and in the fall, I would be attending classes at Southern Arkansas University in Magnolia. I was going to spend the summer at home in Willisville. I was going to plant a garden and walk along the dirt roads, and sing in the church choir again.

I hadn't heard from Abraham since I'd been back in the US. I knew from talking to his mother that he was alive, but that's all she could tell me. He'd sent no letters or messages through his mother or sister—nothing. He hadn't tried to call me, either. I'd given up any hope of ever seeing him again. As hard as it was, I was trying to move on with my life.

"Aunt Bobbie Ann, I'm gonna go outside for a minute," I said.

"Okay, I'm gonna start on dinner in a bit," Aunt Bobbie Ann answered. She was in the kitchen, putting away the groceries she'd bought me. She was doing all she could to make sure I had a good start to my life back home. She would leave to go back to Texas the next morning.

I smiled. "Okay, thank you, but I can cook for myself, you know?"

She returned my smile. "I know. I wanna cook for you."

I gave her a hug. She and Uncle Reggie had been so good to me. Yes, I was upset about Granny handing over guardianship at first, but the two of them becoming my guardians was actually one of the best things that ever happened to me.

I walked outside and sat on the bottom of the front porch. It was early summer and not nearly as hot as it would be as the months stretched on. I knew I'd better enjoy sitting outside while I still could. I sat out there for a long time, watching a squirrel run up and down a pine tree and listening to the crickets chirp and birds sing. I thought about things that never seemed to leave my mind—Maribel, little Marco, the room full of girls, Abraham. There were so many memories—good and bad. There were times when I really missed Mexico. Other times, I was glad I left.

I sat there a while longer, breathing in the scent of honeysuckles and listening to bees buzz. When it started to get dark, I decided to go back inside.

I could smell whatever Aunt Bobbie Ann was cooking and it smelled so good, my stomach started to rumble. I was definitely ready to eat. It was as I turned to walk back into the house that I saw him. He was walking up the dirt road that connected the driveway to the main road. He was still pretty far from the house, but I knew it was him. I knew his walk.

He was wearing jeans and a white t-shirt and he looked thinner. A red baseball cap covered his hair which now hung down his back, almost to his waist. As I stood there and watched him get closer and closer to me, my heart began to pound. Everything was suddenly so quiet, or was it that my loud breathing was drowning everything else out?

He stopped at the edge of the driveway and just stood there and stared. I stared back. And then I smiled at him. Before I could stop myself, I took off running. I ran straight into his arms, wrapping my arms around his neck and my legs around his waist. He laughed. I giggled. My heart was full of everything good in the world—joy, happiness, peace, and love.

He'd found me. He'd kept his word. We were together again just like he said we'd be.

I had no idea what the future held for me and Abraham. But I knew I loved him, I knew he loved me, and I knew he'd take care of me. Maybe I was addicted to loving him like my parents were addicted to drugs and Aunt Bobbie Ann was addicted to alcohol. Or maybe I was just crazy. One thing was for sure; I didn't want to spend another day without him. And right or wrong, we belonged together.

He set me back down on my feet and took my hand. "I'm parked down the road. You ready, angel?"

I looked back at the house where Aunt Bobbie Ann now stood on the front porch, watching us. Then I turned back to Abraham and nodded. "Yes, I'm ready."

Donate to help end Human Trafficking:

http://www.notforsalecampaign.org/donate/

For more information regarding Missing Kids, visit:

http://www.missingkids.com/home

If you think you've seen a missing child, visit the website above or call:

1-800-THE-LOST (1-800-843-5678)

To learn more about Author Adrienne Thompson, visit,
http://adriennethompsonwrites.webs.com

Sign up for Adrienne's newsletter here: http://eepurl.com/jnDmH

Follow Adrienne on Twitter!

https://twitter.com/A_H_Thompson

Like Adrienne on Facebook!

https://www.facebook.com/AdrienneThompsonWrites

Follow Adrienne on Pinterest!

http://www.pinterest.com/ahthompsn/

Also by Adrienne Thompson

The *Bluesday* Series:

Bluesday

Lovely Blues

Blues In The Key Of B

The *Been So Long* Series:

Rapture (A Been So Prequel)

If (Wasif's Story) A Been So Long Prequel – *available exclusively on Adrienne's* website *for FREE*

Been So Long

Little Sister (Cleo's Story—a companion novel to Been So Long)

Been So Long 2 (Body and Soul)

Been So Long III (Whatever It Takes)

Stand-alone novels:

See Me

Your Love Is King

When You've Been Blessed (Feels Like Heaven)

Anthology:

Just Between Us (Inspiring Stories by Women)

Excerpt from *Ain't Nobody*

Coming in 2015

"Are you gonna answer that?" Gwin asked.

I shook my head and pressed the button on my cell phone to reject the call. "Nope."

Gwin sighed. "Okay, it's been three weeks. Haven't you punished him enough?"

"Humph, three weeks versus eight years? I think not."

"Alex, you act like he *made* you stay with him for eight years. That was *your* choice." My best friend was always the voice of reason in my life and she was right. But so was I.

"I know that, but that doesn't mean I have to waste *another* eight years on him. Quincy and I are just not on the same page. Hell, we're not even in the same book."

"Alex, I know you want a family, but is this the way to get it? Are you just gonna punish him until he gives in?"

I wriggled my nose. Why did my nose always choose to itch when I was getting my nails done? "No, I'm done with him. I told you, he was whistling."

She rolled her eyes. "And what does that mean again?"

"It means he'll never marry me. He's happy and satisfied with the way things are and he's not compelled to change them."

"And you got all of that from a whistle?"

I shook my head. "Not just a whistle. Look, I've known this stuff for a while. There have been signs all over the place, but I chose to ignore them. I'm tired of ignoring them now, and I'm tired of Quincy."

"What are you gonna do then?"

I shrugged. "I was gonna take him to Rio for his birthday, but now I think I'll just go by myself and find someone to help me forget about Quincy. Unless you wanna come with me."

Gwin shook her head. "Girl, I'd love to go, but Matt is not gonna let me go to the land of sun and sex without him."

"See, that's what I'm saying. All I want is for someone to care about my comings and goings."

"Quincy cares."

"Whatever."

"Eight years is a lot to throw away."

"Tell Quincy that."

"Alex, you didn't even tell him why you stopped seeing him. Don't you owe him that much?"

I shrugged again.

"Look, you're gonna have to talk to him. If he keeps calling me, my husband's gonna swear we're having an affair."

As if on cue, my phone rang. I looked at Gwin and said, "Okay."

Then I carefully hit the button on my phone and cradled it in my free hand. "Hello, Quincy? Yeah, you need to stop calling Gwin. Her husband is getting upset." I ended the call and slipped my phone into the purse. "There," I said to Gwin.

Gwin's eyes were wide as she said, "That is not what I meant."

I feigned innocence. "Well, what did you mean?"

"Never mind."

Excerpt from *September (The Christina Dandridge Story)*

Coming in 2015

That was the first time she left us behind with relatives. We went to live with our father's mother, Grandma Orene Greene. Grandma Orene was tall and big and dark and downright scary to look at. She looked like she enjoyed whooping kids and those big hands didn't look like they'd show us any mercy if we got out of line. I was so scared when Mama pulled us out of the car and stood us in the yard in front of her, I almost peed on myself.

But then she opened her wide mouth and gave us a smile so warm that I couldn't help but to smile right back at her. Then she started laughing—a big, belly laugh. And I laughed, too.

"Lord, I ain't seen these two babies in so long, I almost forgot how they looked! Beautiful children, they are. Just look at 'em. Just like two little peaches with that orange skin. And those green eyes! Y'all come on over here and give your granny a hug," she gushed.

I was the first to move. I walked over to her and let her wrap her big, heavy warm arms around me. I will never forget how she smelled—like talcum powder and fried chicken. From the moment I met Grandma Orene and felt what it was like to be in her arms, I fell in love with her.

My brother, Kenny Ray, was always shy and I think our grandmother's imposing appearance frightened him a little bit. After she let me go and waited for Kenny to walk over to her, he just stood there with his head hung low. I could tell he was about to cry. My first thought was to call him a cry-baby, and then I realized that he was just four and all he knew was our Mama. He wanted to be with her and so did I. But if she had to leave, I had a feeling we were going to be in good hands with Grandma Orene.

I walked over to my little brother and wrapped my arm around his shoulder. "Come on, Kenny Ray," I whispered. "It's all right."

Mama looked down at him with tears in her eyes. She rubbed her hand over his hair and then squatted down to face him. She pulled him into her arms and whispered, "Be a big boy, Kenny Ray. I'm just going to bring Daddy home. I'll be back before you know it."

Kenny Ray clung tightly to her—cried louder. He didn't believe her. Neither did I. Why would we believe her when the last person who promised to come right back was our daddy? Why would we trust anyone's word at that point?

www.ingramcontent.com/pod-product-compliance
Lightning Source LLC
Chambersburg PA
CBHW070701280626
47159CB00022B/1763